# The Calling

# A

# Novel

# By

# Darren Youngson

# Prologue

John Jones! He was my nemesis – the leader of his juvenile gang at high school. They were always harassing and tormenting students that couldn't defend themselves. And these imbeciles seemed to have a grudge against me and my friend, Pete. It was starting to become a major problem.

One particular cold, damp night, John and his cronies took it into their heads to track us down. They chased us into Craigvinean Forest.

My feet flew over the fallen leaves and there was a moment when I thought that my legs were going to give way. Panic was rising in my chest as I glanced around to see where Pete was, but my fear was worse when he was no where to be seen, but I didn't need to worry about him: it seemed I was the one who was their centre of attention.

My eyes fell on a gap at the base of a tree. I threw myself at it, trying not to give away my position as leaves crunched under my feet. Just as they were in sight, I peeked out to observe their next move.

There were four of them standing in the distance looking in each and every direction. One skinny small-boned, blond boy with a Glaswegian accent, Paul, took off his baseball cap to have a better scan of the area. The other two were twins, Frank and Jesse, who obviously shared similar features as well as character traits – one was as dumb as the other. Their hair was beach-blond and their bodies chubby in stature which caused them both to wheeze at the slightest hint of exercise. Their persona made me think that they'd be a success in show business or some sort of comedy routine where audiences could point and laugh at how pathetic they were.

As for John, well, to his compadres, he was known as Jonesy. He was a rough-looking boy, with constant mischief in his eyes. Trouble stalked him everywhere he went and the others followed.

'Come on out, Jacob, we're going to find you sooner or later. If not here then at school,' Jonesy's voice reverberated throughout the forest.

'Fuck this, man, am going hame for a munch. Face it, Jonesy, he's gone,' Paul said, wiping the sweat off his brow and putting his cap back on.

'Shut the fuck up. We'll find that little shit.'

They turned their backs to me and, as I watched them walk away, I decided to make a run for it.

'There he is!' a voice exclaimed.

I ran as fast as I could, focusing on the path that lay before me.

But judging by the sounds of their voices, they'd clearly fanned out. I heard verbal expletives followed by rapid breathing as my pursuers endeavoured to catch me. I manoeuvred myself from tree-to-tree to help compromise their vision; the trees were thick enough to provide cover. I made a bid for the next trunk. I was almost there when a body flew out and knocked me off my feet. Paul and I fell to the ground.

'We've got you now, you little shit. HEY, GUYS, I'VE GOT HIM!' he shouted.

Soon after the rest of my pursuers arrived at the scene. Frank and Paul took hold of my arms as I struggled to get free and pull them back. I dug my feet into the mulch, pressing my back against a tree. The pain shooting up my arms was unbearable; I looked at Frank and Paul's grinning faces as they pulled from each side.

Jonesy walked up to me until we were face to face. His smile was menacing; he gave out a small chuckle and said, 'You're gonna pay for what you did in the school toilets, you little cunt.'

'I had no choice,' I said.

He threw a punch to my stomach. The air burst free from my lungs as his fist made contact. Tears filled my eyes. I couldn't breathe. A hand yanked my hair back so that my throat was exposed. The adrenaline channelling through my body was more profound as Jonesy pulled out a knife. An uncontrollable rage built up in me and I felt myself changing.

'Jonesy, please don't do this!' I begged, but they paid no heed to my words. They weren't going to listen.

I was past the point of no return. The transformation was triggered by instinct, somehow sensing danger and acting as, I could only guess, a self-defence mechanism.

They punched and kicked me, but as the beating progressed, pain was no longer a factor; I was resilient to their attacks. My body started to increase in size as my bones snapped and altered.

The feeling of my antagonist's limbs making contact with my body stopped short as they were witnessing my clothes ripping to expose fur. And just as my body mass increased, I felt Jonesy's knife penetrate one of my ribs, but the blade simply slipped back out and fell to the ground as the growing commenced.

Shocked faces greeted me as I stood up, snarling to expose teeth and I poised myself with claws outstretched ready to slash. I regarded my awestruck antagonists who seemed paralytic with fear. There was a momentarily silence between them and the beast I'd become. Then, an abrupt roar left my mouth, almost deafening to my own ears, echoing around the quiet forest and disturbing the wildlife.

**1**

It was the year of 1985 and my parents, Helen and Robert Ferguson, were blessed with myself. According to my parents (when they mentioned this to me at a later age), they thought it unusual that my body-developmental skills progressed at such an early stage. Curious as they were, they decided to consult a general practitioner for advice.

'He's probably one of the first infants to reach the ambulatory state at an early age,' was all he said.

So, in addition, my first steps occurred around the age of three months and eventually I was a proficient walker by the fourth.

My first word occurred around the same time, but my parents thought nothing of it and by that, I mean they didn't find it odd after the doctor's analysis. They were just overwhelmed and ecstatic I said the word that appeared to sound like "Mum".

The adolescent years were awkward and puberty started to kick in during the end of my primary school years. I thought nothing of it; my naïveness made me think of it all as part of growing up, so I didn't know any better. My parents were kind and caring but were bothered about certain individuals finding my so-called "condition" uncanny. But most comments mentioned the fact that my face should be on magazine covers – it was a story people wanted. But my parents only wanted a quiet life.

Those early years of growing up in the small tranquil town of Newburgh were in fact, peaceful. The only hard part was (and I believe that other young individuals would agree) primary school. Due to the changes I was going through, it was not easy having children ridiculing my appearance. They pointed and laughed at the hair under my armpits and made fun of my voice due to its distortion.

I stood there on a hot summer's day, waiting for lunch to end. I always ate alone and I was itching to get back to class, so I was in teachers' eye-sight. Being around teachers made me feel safe from the other kids, but unfortunately, the rules were that you weren't allowed inside the school building during lunch.

As I stood at the main doors waiting for the bell to signify the end of lunch, I felt hands on my back, pushing me full force to the ground. Multiple laughs came roaring from kids' mouths as they witnessed the shove. My elbow ached and my hand was grazed. I tried not to cry as I looked up at my assailant.

'Ha, ha. How was your trip?' a young Jonesy said as he looked down at me, his hair tousled and dried mud clinging to his trousers and hands. Laughs and sarky comments came from the other kids. I could see Jonesy was thriving on it.

He was the one that got to me the most. I didn't ever see him without a frightening, hostile expression on his face, and his scruffy, worn clothes made his appearance worse. It looked as though they could be ripped clean off with one simple grasp. All in all, he had the appearance of a homeless kid.

Before Jonesy could continue his malice, a young, smart-looking boy came to my aid; he wore a pair of dark framed glasses, his hair was neatly combed and he was dressed in a pair of well-ironed trousers and shirt that had the primary school logo attached to the left hand side of the chest.

'Leave him alone!' the boy said in an English accent.

Jonesy's gaze shifted from me to the English boy. 'What you going to do about it, Pete?' he said, walking towards him.

Pete's body language was tentative and shaky as Jonesy stood in front of him. 'I said, what are you going to do about it?'

Pete didn't answer; he just stood with his head down, staring at the ground sheepishly.

'I'm telling the headmaster on you,' I said.

Jonesy focused his attention back to me, 'Listen to you, you sound weird. Why are you such a freak, Jacob?'

'If you don't leave us alone, I'll tell on you,' I threatened once again.

Jonesy's hands waved in the air and he mimed crying. 'Oh... I'm sorry. Please don't tell on me, I'm really scared. I'll leave you two freaks alone.'

He went back to Pete, but before he could do anything, my anger kicked in, 'Why don't you just fuck off!'

Some of the kids backed off from my sudden outburst and others walked away still giggling as the school bell rang.

Lunch time was at an end. 'This isn't over, freak,' he said and delivered a punch to my stomach before walking away to class.

Once more, I found myself on the ground trying to breathe

as the young English boy approached me and introduced himself.

'Are you all right?'

I nodded.

'I'm Peter by the way, but you can call me Pete.' He seemed oddly polite and intelligent for a boy his age. My only thoughts were that his parents were either wealthy and had given him the right education or he was more of a self-learner.

I introduced myself as my breath came back. I knew it was the start of a good friendship. And, furthermore, I guessed we had something in common… we were both outcasts.

He told me how he'd moved to Scotland from England a year ago and that most of his family had already moved to Scotland and loved it, so encouraged his parents to move closer.

'What's Jonesy's problem?' I asked.

'Don't know,' Pete said, 'but he's picked on me since I started at this school.'

'Should we tell on him?'

Pete chewed his lip, 'Better not.'

'Why?'

'Cause last time I told on him he done something bad to me.'

'What did he do?'

Pete remained silent for a moment then told me his story.

*I was in class, but desperately needed to go to the bathroom. I couldn't wait any longer, I was too fidgety on my chair which caught the teacher's attention. 'Peter, do you need to go to the toilet?'*

*'Yes, Miss.'*

*'Then I suggest you go, and be quick about it.'*

*She turned her attention back to the blackboard, and continued her lesson as I rushed out the door.*

*It felt like forever getting to the toilet, but as I entered, there were two boys skiving. One was Jonesy, the other, a blond boy named Paul.*

*Paul was sitting next to the sinks. Jonesy just stood there looking at me, amused by the sight of my squint posture as I held in my pee.*

*They both approached. 'It's the English wee fanny,' Paul said.*

*Jonesy noticed my hands against my groin and put two and two together. 'What's wrong? Need the toilet, Pete?'*

*I couldn't speak, I was shit scared and was close to peeing myself. I needed to go desperately, but Jonesy took care of that problem. He threw a punch to my lower stomach. I fell to the ground and my pee flowed uncontrollably.*

*They both laughed as I wept at the wet patch on my school trousers.*

*'Aw, did you have a wee accident?' Paul said.*

*Paul seemed satisfied at the loss of my dignity, but Jonesy wasn't done. He opened one of the cubicle doors. 'Don't worry, Pete. We'll help you get cleaned up, right, Paul?*

*Paul seemed puzzled, but eventually got the hint.*

*They both grabbed me by the arms and forced me into one of the cubicles. I tried to resist as my head was getting closer to the toilet bowl. Eventually, my face came in contact with pissy water. I tried to move it upwards but a hand stopped it. It held me down. Bubbles exploded as the air left my lungs. I thought I was going to drown there and then.*

*I felt my body go limp, and as hands were released, I fell over to the side of the toilet. They both just walked away with laughter. 'Catch you later, Pete.'*

*I don't know how long I laid there next to that stinking toilet. What do you do when something like that happens? I couldn't go back to class as the smell would make things complicated, not to mention I'd be the laughing stock for years on end.*

I knew it couldn't have been easy for Pete to confess his story to me. So I didn't say anything. We both stood in silence for a moment. I could see his lips tremble as the images of that frightful day came back to him.

'What do you do when that happens?' he said.

'Didn't you tell anyone?'

'I went straight to the school nurse and said I had an accident. She knew something was amiss just by looking at me. She cleaned me up and I was allowed to go home. I guess she wanted to save me from the embarrassment.'

'What did your mum and dad say?'

'They got in touch with the headmaster, and things led to Jonesy being suspended. But that only made him worse. He keeps annoying me – beating me up or calling me names – him and his friends. I hate them!'

Pete wiped his tears away and eventually gathered his composure. We both went back to class, but he still seemed puzzled.

As we walked, I couldn't help but notice his attention towards me. 'What?' I asked.

The look he gave me was more curious than strange. 'Sorry for staring, it's just odd.'

'What is?' I asked.

'Well, it's just your voice; we're in primary school and your voice seems deeper than any of the other students. You just seem different. Are you on some sort of hormonal medication or something?'

I didn't understand what he meant; I didn't even know what hormonal was. So I just nodded and said, 'I guess.' He broke into a smile and laughed at me; he clearly knew I didn't understand what he was saying.

We got to know each other during the rest of the school hours; we laughed and played games while keeping out of Jonesy's sight. We bonded well and I felt a sense of relief now that I wasn't completely alone during my school years and I could tell Pete felt the same way. I'd made a friend but I'd also made an enemy.

## 2

School had finished, but I wasn't too eager to leave after witnessing Jonesy up ahead in the corridor. I slowed my pace and tried to blend in with the other kids to keep out of his sight.

My house wasn't too far from the school, but Pete needed to get a bus that took him to the outskirts of Newburgh.

At last! Jonesy was on the bus and I felt a sudden rush of relief as it moved off. I walked home undisturbed, yet my mind couldn't relax considering I'd have to repeat this same performance the next day, and the next, and so forth.

Lost in my own world, I found myself almost home. My head shot up at the sound of voices. Dad was standing at the front door, talking to a man, but his body language showed that he was pretty angry.

The closer I got, the more I could hear my dad's furious tone. He was shouting at this stranger, who, strangely enough, seemed calm. His clothing appeared casual; he wore a pair of denim jeans and a white T-shirt. His body language and hand gestures were expressive and had a somewhat explanatory attitude towards them. Was he trying to sell something? Was he a Jehovah's Witness? If so, I didn't think it necessary for Dad to shout down his throat. He could have just said "No thanks" and closed the door on him like an ordinary, civilized human being.

I didn't hear much of the conversation, but it became more audible the closer I got. By eavesdropping out of sight, I could hear fragments, but some of the stranger's words were too odd to comprehend. But I understood the words "your son".

As the strange man was told where to go by an aggressive Dad, I casually walked towards the gate. The man's eyes made contact with me. I couldn't help notice he appeared to be expressing a sense of joy and wonderment as his gaze fell upon me. And it seemed like he had the urge to interact with me but was disturbed by Dad's abrupt tone. 'Come inside, Jacob.'

'But, Dad, I—'

'Now!'

Dad and I watched this man with an awestruck fascination as he walked away. 'Who was that?' I asked.

'You'd better come in, son. We need to talk.'

My nerves were running wild. Was the man someone from school who'd come to pay a visit to my house because he wasn't happy with my progress?

We took a seat in the living room. Mum was also present; her eyes were red and I could tell she'd been crying.

'What's going on? Am I in trouble?' I asked.

There was a slight tension between them both. They regarded each other then Dad sat next to me, took a deep breath and spoke. 'Jacob, eh… have you ever heard the word adoption before?'

I nodded.

He became tongue-tied as the words battled to leave his mouth; I didn't understand what he was trying to say, but he found his words after a slight hesitation. 'Before you were born, your mother and I tried to… eh… have a child, but it was impossible for us.'

Dad was now on the edge of his seat. His gaze shifted from me to Mum as he reluctantly tried to explain what he was trying to say.

I felt bad for not understanding as Dad sat there, fiddling with his fingers and staring at the floor.

'Adoption means, eh…' he was obviously trying to think of his words carefully, 'adoption means that when two people are in love and can't have a baby of their own, they are able to take care of someone else's child.'

'Is that bad?' I asked in bewilderment.

'No, no. It's a good thing. It's just some people under certain circumstances are unable to take care of their child and have to give them up for adoption. And that's what adoption means.

'What I'm trying to say is that you're adopted, Jacob.'

I was still puzzled at this. 'Then, who are my real parents?' was all I said.

'We are, Jacob,' Mum said, with a tremble in her voice. She sat opposite me; her brunette, long hair was dishevelled as she fumbled with a handkerchief that looked wet from tears. She was beside herself as she continued to speak. 'We were so delighted when we got the call from the hospital—'

'Yes, but there's more to the story,' Dad interrupted.

'Robert, no!' Mum protested. 'He doesn't need to know the rest, it sickens me.'

Dad put a hand up to silence her. 'Helen, please, it's better now than never. He needs to hear this.'

She sat back in her chair with a sigh, defeated.

Dad continued, 'When we arrived at the hospital, we were overjoyed as we held you in our arms, but one of the nurses had a strange story to tell of how they obtained you. She was outside on a smoking break when her eyes caught sight of a strange figure stumbling towards the hospital entrance, carrying something. The figure placed this object down near the doors and ran off. She hurried to investigate. The object was a few blankets intertwined with one another and they were moving. She opened them to behold a healthy infant, and a torn piece of paper inside with the word "Jacob" written on it. She said you didn't even cry as you were left there on that cold, rainy night.'

Dad took a moment and waited for me to speak, but what could a ten-year-old kid say to that? How should a boy react when they've just heard they were adopted? 'I don't understand,' was my only reply.

'You don't have to understand, son. I just thought I'd tell you now. We couldn't make any sense of it either. We asked questions to see if it was one of your real parents that left you there, but the staff at the hospital were just as dumbfounded as we were, so we put it at the back of our minds. We're telling you this now because we didn't want you to be mad with us at a later age or to hear it from someone else.'

There was a momentarily silence as my mind tried to process this information, but I didn't know how to. I eventually spoke, 'No, I'm not mad, Dad.'

A half-smile formed on his lips, and he appeared to be a bit more relaxed now that that was off his chest. 'We just thought it was best to hear it from us rather than that man you just saw.'

'Who was he?' I asked.

'He claimed to know your real parents. But it doesn't matter; he's just a mad man. Best to keep away from him. And if you can, put it at the back of your mind.'

'What happens if he comes back?'

Dad looked at Mum again and to ease her nerves said, 'We're going to phone the police. Just in case.'

## 3

Later that night the police were at my house. Dad was confident at explaining the situation but Mum appeared to be hysterical. She asked questions like, 'What if he kidnaps him? What if he tries to hurt him or worse?'

'Helen, please!' was Dad's response. 'Will you stop jumping to conclusions and let me explain to the officers.' He looked back at them. They were standing in front of the television that wasn't on. I stood beside Mum, feeling intimidated by the man and woman in uniform.

One introduced himself as Officer Gregory. His size was frightening to me but his face was friendly and his attitude was patient. 'And this is my colleague, Officer Michaelson.' Michaelson stood there with a notepad and pen but she didn't just follow protocol; she seemed like a compassionate woman with concern in her eyes while listening to Dad's statement.

He mentioned as vividly as possible the man's size, hair colour and what he was wearing. His mannerisms were calm but I could tell as I sat there next to Mum he was nervous. Gregory asked the questions as Michaelson took notes with her pencil, occasionally touching her lips with it in concentration.

As Mum comforted me I couldn't help but think *am I going to get into trouble if I report this man? Will he be mad after the police question him and go on a revenge spree and hurt us, maybe even kill us?*

A good hour or so had passed and the two police officers looked like they had all the details they'd required. But something happened; it was something Gregory had done. Not sure if it was professional or he was just thinking outside the box. He looked at me, took his hat off and kneeled down to my level as I sat on the couch with Mum.

'How are you feeling, son?' he asked.

My head was lowered, 'Fine, sir,' I said as I fiddled with my hands.

'Quite polite.' Gregory looked around as he said this which caused a small chuckle around the room. He knew I was afraid of the entire situation but he gave some advice which was slightly comforting.

'Don't worry, kid, your parents will take care of you. If you're out and about, let's say after school or playing with friends, make sure you're in a place where there's lots of people.

'If by chance you do see this man again while on your own, run away and tell the nearest person in sight and tell your mum and dad. Okay?'

'Yes, sir,' was my only reply.

The Inspector giggled and tousled my hair which put a small smile on my face.

Mum and Dad looked impressed by his comforting manner-isms. He stood up, put his hat back on and said, 'We'll be in touch. Like I said: if there's anything else – any hint of the man –  just call the police immediately.' Both officers gave a reassuring smile and left, Mum and Dad thanking them.

After a long day of strange events and reminiscing about my past, I decided to go to bed, but that was no easy task either. The conversation with my parents left me with thoughts that raced round and round. Maybe I was thinking too much into it but Dad was right: I should put it to the back of my mind and try and forget about it. But why would anyone claiming to know my biological parents come to my door? Surely it wasn't a coincidence. Eventually, I fell asleep, but my slumber was restless; I tossed and turned, falling into a vivid dream.

As it progressed, it manifested itself into a nightmare. The environment around me was dark and gloomy. I felt myself running and panting as if being chased by an unknown being. My view was focused on a vague white light in front of me in the distance. As I ran, the light became larger. My gaze shifted behind to my rear view. Deep in the inky-black centre of this dream world, there was a form, a shape of some kind, that appeared indistinguishable. This silhouette stood erect, swiftly moving in my direction; it was coming for me. I couldn't make out its features, but I came to the conclusion that it was a man, though it didn't seem human.

The light in front of me was now larger than before. I tried to turn my run into a sprint towards sanctuary and yet it still felt as if the dark silhouette was pulling me back with an unfathomable force. A scream left my mouth, but there was no sound. You can put so much effort into a dream or nightmare, but, in the end, the bogeyman still prevails.

I looked behind me again to figure out the dark silhouette's position. He was getting closer, and as he did, his shape and form started to change. He became taller until the whole outline of his body had a non-human appearance to it. This thing that supposedly used to be a man now growled and sniffed as it tried to hunt me down. After another quick, curious glance, I could make out some of its features from its dark shadowed body. Two pointy tips protruded at each side of the head. The hands held multiple sharp objects which, to me, appeared to be blades.

I was nearing the light, but the creature was poised. With magnificent speed and swift movement, it executed a sprint-and-leap. As I approached the light that felt like a way out of this hell, the creature was on me. It snarled, bit and slashed as I watched the light fade and the dream world was encumbered in complete darkness.

I woke up with a scream. My bed was drenched with sweat and I was panting. Mum quickly came into the room; she saw me sobbing with my knees against my chest and immediately knew it was a bad dream.

She sat next to me and comforted me, 'Shh. It's okay, son.'

'It was a monster!'

'Whatever it was, it's gone now. It was just a bad dream you had.'

I tried to wipe the dream from my mind there and then, but the horrible, profound feeling of the aftermath remained. Mum took me in her arms; she stroked my head, rocked me back and forth and my night ended with her tranquil voice singing me a lullaby that eventually pacified my excitement and sent me into a restful sleep.

## 4

## Pete

It was summer time! I rode my bicycle enjoying the sun as I cycled towards Jacob's house. The road was quiet which was to be expected on a Sunday afternoon. I could still hear Mum's voice in my head, 'Wear your helmet, Peter. Take a jacket with you in case it rains.' But there was no rain, and I certainly wasn't going to wear a helmet. Too dorky!

I arrived just in time to see Jacob and his dad fiddling with his bike. 'Hey, Jacob!' His head bobbed up as I performed a skid at his gate.

'Easy there, Peter. You might have an accident,' Mr Ferguson said.

'Sorry, Mr Ferguson.'

'It's alright, but you should be wearing a helmet – and call me Robert.'

'Will do, Mr Ferguson – Robert.'

Robert sighed and went into the house as I approached Jacob. 'What you been up to?'

'Nothing much. Just making sure everything's fine with my bike. My dad helped me straighten the handle bars as they were a bit squint. He also put some oil on the chain.'

'Cool. You ready?'

Jacob turned his attention towards my head. 'Where is your helmet?'

'Not you as well. Jeez, you sound like my mum.'

We both laughed then went on our way, but not before Jacob was stopped short by his dad. 'Jacob!' He stood at the door holding a grey helmet.

'Aw, Dad.'

'No. You have to wear it for your own good. Mother's orders.'

'Hey, don't blame me.' a voice came from within the house. Jacob's mum came outside and stood next to Robert.

'Just following your orders, honey,' Robert said with a chuckle.

'We both agree to the same rules, Robert. Don't make me the bad guy here.'

She looked at the helmet then at Jacob. 'Jacob, wear the helmet.'

He reluctantly put it on. 'Happy now?'

'Attaboy,' they both said humorously. 'Now, remember, Jacob, don't talk to any strangers,' Robert's voice was serious. 'You understand?'

'Yes,' Jacob said impatiently.

'You must be careful who you talk to just like what we discussed.'

'I know, I know. Can I go now?' Jacob asked as he was eager to get out the gate.

'Yeah, of course.'

We both cycled off. 'Bye, bye, you two. Have fun.'

'What was that all about?' I asked.

'Nothing. Let's just go.'

He seemed angry by the performance of his mum and dad's parental skills. 'Your mum's kind of hot,' I said just to lighten the mood.

He looked at me as we pedalled. 'Shut up.'

The sun was beating down on our backs as we rode towards the small country roads. We stopped next to a farmhouse that was connected to a straight road leading outwards towards the city of Dundee.

We stood and leaned against a wall to catch our breath. The open fields were breathtaking; we could make out the River Tay in the distance, and up ahead, trees stood erect as if welcoming us towards their domain, but the only thing spoiling the tranquillity was the smell of manure.

It was peaceful; not a car or body in sight. I looked at the long stretch of road and smiled, 'Fancy a race?'

Jacob studied the road ahead, 'Okay, sure.'

We both lined up our bikes so we were parallel with one another. Jacob tightened the strap on his helmet. *Dork.*

'On your marks… Get set… GO!'

We were off. The wind blew against our faces as I pedalled to overtake Jacob. He was struggling to keep up. He strived to keep up with me, let alone take over. He wasn't even looking where he was going; he just looked down at his legs as if encouraging them to move faster.

'Come on, you'll have to do better than that.'

His only reply was the sound of his panting.

Finally, I reached the end of the road and finished with a skid. 'I win!'

'Asshole,' Jacob said breathlessly. 'Your bike is faster than mine.'

'Excuses, excuses.'

'How did you get so fast?'

'Cause I'm better than you.'

We both laughed then sat on the grass on the verge. A question puzzled me, so I asked out of the blue, 'What did your dad mean about strangers?'

'What'd you mean? Every parent's always on about strangers.' Jacob said. However, it felt as though he was avoiding the question.

'It was just the way how he went on about it.'

He didn't seem too keen to explain. He rubbed the sweat from his forehead then eventually explained.

'A man visited my house, didn't know who he was, but I think he's related to me.'

'Okay… What happened?' I asked.

'Well, my dad and the man were arguing. Just before the man walked away, he gave this strange look, but that's not the worst part. Get this, apparently I'm adopted.'

I couldn't believe what Jacob told me. Who would of thought my best friend was adopted. It didn't really matter though. I wiped the condensation from my glasses, 'Is that a bad thing?'

Jacob picked a bit of grass and fiddled with it. 'I don't know. It feels strange knowing my real parents gave me up for adoption –'

'But you already have real parents, Jacob! What does it matter? You've always known your mum and dad, right?'

'I guess.'

'Well then, there's nothing to worry about.'

Jacob looked at me and smiled, 'Thanks, Pete. How do you know about this stuff?'

I smiled, 'I read a lot.' I stood up, wiped the grass from my behind and said, 'Let's go get an ice-cream. It's too hot out here.'

We both grabbed our bikes, and I asked for another race but Jacob declined. 'Pete,' he uttered before I was about to take off, 'don't tell anyone.'

'Sure.'

'I mean it – not even your parents.'

'I promise.'


It was just after 3pm; it seemed as though the sun was still at its zenith. The heat at Newburgh High Street was unbearable; you could even see it bouncing off the tarmac. I couldn't wait to get an ice-cream in me, I'm sure Jacob felt the same.

Vanessa's Ice-Cream Shop was right in the middle of town. The shop only had a few tables and chairs outside, and they were vacant. Thank God. I was needing a break from the bike. We parked them on the right next to the shop door. Jacob took off his helmet and hung it on one of the handle bars. 'You look like a dork,' I said.

'Better safe than sorry.'

We walked in and there was Vanessa finishing off serving a customer. She was hot: nice smile, dark hair and big boobs.

'Hi, Vanessa,' I waved with a big smile on my face.

'Hi, Vanessa,' Jacob mimicked.

I gave him a shove. 'Shut up.'

'Hey, you two. You boys behaving yourselves?'

'No,' we said in unity.

She laughed. 'What will it be then?'

'Usual for me,' I said.

'Mint with a chocolate cone?'

'That's the one,' I said while trying to contain my smile.

'Just chocolate for me with a plain cone.'

'No probs, Jacob.'

It only took a few minutes for her to get it ready. When she was done I paid for us both, 'Thank you…' My smile was released once more, and Vanessa giggled.

'Pete.'

'What.'

'My ice-cream,' Jacob said impatiently.

'Oh, yeah, sorry.' I passed it to him and we left the shop. 'Bye, Vanessa.'

Vanessa giggled again, 'Bye. Stay out of trouble.'

'Okay.'

The ice-cream was soothing against our tongues as we made our way to the seats outside, but our pleasure was soon changed to dread. Sitting at the table was Jonesy. Paul was there too with two other boys who were twins. Their bikes were scattered haphazardly against the shop wall.

Jonesy's back was towards us; it was Paul and the twins that saw us. 'Look who it is, the English fanny and a little knob.'

'You two make a perfect couple,' one of the twins said.

Jonesy turned then stood up. He walked towards us without a word, clearly knowing our paralysis could be used to his advantage. I felt the ice-cream melt and drip cold streams down my hand, but had no reaction.

'Your ice-cream's melting,' Jonesy said.

My eyes looked down at my hand, but I abruptly felt the coldness of the cream splat against my face. An outburst of laughter followed as I wiped away the cold liquid from my eyes. They were all cheering Jonesy on like cheerleaders rooting for their team.

Jacob just stood there as I cleaned myself, his eyes on Jonesy. His hand that held the ice-cream was trembling, and his jaw was clenched. Out of nowhere he managed to sum up a bit courage and, unexpectedly, Jonesy was now suffering the same fate as I had as Jacob shoved his ice-cream in his face all the way to the end of the cone.

It was fight or flight. Without a thought Jacob and I grabbed our bikes, inadvertently taking the wrong ones; he had mine and vice versa. We took off, but Jacob's helmet fell off the bike during the process. Jonesy and the others followed, clumsily picking up their own bikes with frustration, screaming expletives which turned curious eyes.

We had a head start, but the boys quickly caught up, probably because they were fitter than us or slightly older.

Our bums were off the seat to give us that extra push. I looked back; Jonesy was in the lead of the others. His white dripping face and exposed clenched teeth made him look like a maniacal ghost rider. His legs moved rapidly as they worked the pedals. 'I'm going to fucking kill you!'    Roads were still quiet; the odd car passed by and honked their horns as we were a hindrance to them. I saw people nodding their heads in shame and mouthing things to us, but the wind was hitting my ears hard so I couldn't make out what it was. Our adrenaline was working tenfold; we panted as sweat ran down our bodies, causing our clothes to stick to our skin. I didn't know how long I could've kept this up, but somehow the thought of being chased by a pursuer kept me going.

Jacob, surprisingly, was keeping up. In fact he was slightly ahead of me as we approached the bottom of the high street. I quickly looked behind to check on our pursuers; they were now parallel with one another with faces of rage. I kind of feared for my life.

The chase led us back onto the more quieter roads; not many places to hide, and not many places to ride as Jacob and I were done. Jacob's house was too far; so was mine. We had to find a place of safety.

The boys were right behind us. I saw the twins extend their arms as they tried to take hold of me or cause me to lose balance. Jacob was ahead (I guess my bike *was* faster) but Jonesy whooshed past me.

'Jacob!' I exclaimed.

He looked back at my warning and noticed Jonesy coming up behind. Jonesy manoeuvred until they were side by side. Jacob put his head down again to probably say to his legs to move faster, but it seemed their speed was both equally matched. Both individual's legs were now going through a rapid frenzy; it looked more like a race than a chase.

I don't know if Jonesy was becoming fatigued but it seemed Jacob was speeding up. Way up! His feet moved with such tremendous speed that it was hard to distinguish they were feet at all. They were just a blur to the naked eye.

Paul and the twins focused their attention towards the chase, puzzled and awestruck by Jacob's performance, but it was over as soon as it began. Jacob was miraculously too fast for my bike. His sudden burst of speed made the chain snap, causing him to lose his footing. The bike then lost control, and Jacob crashed onto the verge with it bouncing slightly ahead of him, causing Jonesy to edge slightly ahead.

I approached with the other three boys, their mischievous ways alleviated by this new turn of events as their attention was focused on Jacob.

Jonesy turned round, came back and stopped with a skid next to Jacob. 'You might be fast, you little shit, but you can't run forever.' He spat on him then joined the others that still held awestruck faces then rode off. I guessed they'd thought Jacob had had enough for one day. He was a mess: blood trickled down his face (where a helmet would've came in handy), knees were scraped and his right hand had a nasty gash across the palm.

The journey back home wasn't a pleasant one. My bike was in a bad state: broken chain, slightly bent tire and the handle bars were squint. It wasn't easy but I had to carry it home. Jacob walked with his own bike; with each step he let out a gasp of pain. 'Sorry about your bike,' he said.

'It's fine. I just want to know what happened back there?'

'What do you mean?'

'Your speed. I knew my bike was fast, but that was something else. You could've won that race we had.'

Jacob laughed but let out a moan. He checked his hand which now held dried blood, his sleeve also held a crimson streak as he wiped the wound on his head. 'I just wanted to go fast so I did.'

Still puzzled and left with questions, I thought better not to ask and focused on getting us home as the day's final moments were stressful.

Jacob's parents were sitting outside their house enjoying the last few hours of the sun. Helen was the first to rush towards him. 'Oh, my God! What happened?'

Jacob looked at me apprehensively. 'We had a race,' I said. 'Jacob lost his balance and fell.'

'Didn't you wear your helmet like we said?'

He was tongue-tied so I filled in for him. 'He gave it to me, but I lost it.'

'How the hell do you lose a helmet?' It was Robert that stepped in. I just shrugged my shoulders and admitted defeat.

'And why's your bike in a state, Peter?'

'We swapped bikes.'

Both parents just nodded with disappointment. 'Honestly, you kids, these days…' Robert rambled on as he went inside to fetch his car keys. He came back out, 'Well, I might as well give you a lift home, Peter. Can't let you walk home with that,' he pointed to my bike, 'on your shoulder.'

'And you, young man,' it was Helen's turn, 'get inside so I can clean you up. What a state you're in.'

'Yes, Mum.'

'I'll see you later, Jacob.'

'Catch you later, Pe–' Jacob's mum slammed the door before he could finish.

The initial row was over for Jacob, but I had to face my own parents now. Robert parked the car, got out and took the bike from the boot. The car journey was an awkward silence, but as we walked to my door I apologised to him. 'It's alright, Peter. We've all been kids at some point. We learn from our mistakes so try to be a bit more responsible next time.'

I nodded and remained silent but Robert spoke again. 'Now this won't be easy, but your mum and dad are probably going to be mad.'

'I know.'

'Just swallow it up, and take it.'

I was silent again, Robert's advice gave me a bit of respect for him. He's telling it like he's been through the same. After all, like he said, "We've all been kids at some point".

Robert knocked.

It was Mum that came to the door, puzzled by Robert's presence then she saw the bike. 'What happened?'

Robert spoke for me. 'It's alright, Margaret, just a little hiccup. My son and Peter swapped bikes. Unfortunately, Jacob crashed this one.'

'Oh. Is he alright?'

'Just some cuts and bruises. But I promise I'll pay for the damage.'

'Don't be daft, Robert,' Dad said as he came to the door. 'This'll come straight out of Peter's pocket money.' Dad then turned his attention to me, 'You got anything to say?'

'They were just having fun on a summer's day, Mike,' Robert said.

'Maybe, but money doesn't grow on trees. That bike was expensive. You get in that house and straight to your room.'

I walked in with my head down. Robert and my parents had a quick chat about our behaviour, thanked him for bringing me home then he left.

Mum and Dad stood at my room door, shouting their heads off at me. I just had to ride through it. They wouldn't let this situation slide anytime soon. I just hoped Jacob was doing better than I was.

## 5

Jacob

I sat on my bed staring down at my legs. Mum done a good job of cleaning up my wounds, and I felt a bit better after a bath. Her hands were gentle but her mouth kept rambling on about how stupid Pete and I were. 'Why did you swap bikes? Why did you lose your helmet?' Blah, blah, blah. The thing I focused on though was what went wrong with Pete's bike? Was it the bike? What was that momentarily burst of speed I'd possessed? I didn't know how to tell Mum or Dad what'd happened – doubtful they would understand.

Later, Mum came into my room. She seemed more at ease now she'd got her anger out while nursing my wounds. 'Are you okay, son?'

'Fine, Mum.' She saw the look I gave her, and the flood gates opened.

'Jacob, what's wrong?' She sat on the bed next to me – comforting me as I sobbed on her chest.

'Boys!' I sniffed.

'Boys? Boys at school?'

I nodded, and wiped away tears.

'Jacob, are you being bullied?'

I nodded again.

'What's going on?' Dad said as he came into the room.

'There's boys at school hassling, Jacob.'

Dad knelt in front of me. He looked at my plasters, 'Were these boys the cause of this?'

I sniffed again, 'Yeah. They chased us, and that's how I fell.'

'Is Peter getting bullied as well?' Dad asked.

'Yeah.'

Dad stood up with Mum looking at him. 'Is this happening in school and out?'

I nodded.

'Well, we're going to have to do something about this.'

'Like what, Robert? It's summer time, the schools are shut. Maybe their parents–'

'No!' I exclaimed. 'Don't call their parents.'

'Why not?' Mum asked puzzled.

'It'll only make Jonesy mad.'

'Jonesy?' Mum said, still puzzled.

'That's his name.'

'But surely–'

'No, no. Jacob's right, Helen. We can aggravate these boys even more, causing hell for Jacob and Peter.'

'Robert, come on.'

'No. He's right. Bully helplines. The talk with their parents and headmaster – it gets you nowhere.'

'Robert, where is this coming from?'

Dad paced the room then stared off into space. 'I was bullied, severely, at high school.

'What did you do?' I was curious.

He looked at me with a smile, 'After all the talk with teachers and parents failed, I turned to a lot of Kung-Fu movies and learnt a few tricks or two.

I was impressed, 'Cool.'

'Not really.' He turned and faced us. 'It didn't end well.'

'You never mentioned this.' Mum was now acting like Dad was the victim.

'It's part of my life I'm trying to forget.' Dad sat on my computer chair with his head down probably reliving those memories. We sat in silence waiting for him to continue, but he remained silent.

Mum broke the silence, 'Well, we have to do something. How long for the holidays to end: two weeks?'

Dad nodded.

'Then we'll get in touch with the school when Jacob goes back. In the meantime I'm going to phone Peter's parents. It's too late to do it now so I'll phone first thing in the morning. Surely there's something we can do?'

He smiled incredulously. 'Okay, Helen. Let's do it your way.'


Pete

I lay on my bed reading, trying to distract my mind from the events that happened the day before. It seemed Jonesy has made new friends – those weird looking twins. What happened if he gained more followers? He could have an alliance. Bullies do what they do best when others bully to fit in. If you can't beat them, join them, I guessed.

Unfortunately, Jacob and I were their targets. How did you solve that kind of predicament? Did you take out the leader rendering the others powerless? How to do that was beyond me.

I gave up on the book, put it away in my bedside cabinet and stared up at the ceiling. The dull day didn't help my mood. Drops of rain clashed against my window as I got up and looked outside. I wanted to do something creative in the outside world regardless of the rain, but the thought of Jonesy was off putting. The other thing that was puzzling me was Jacob. That speed! It was phenomenal. Who could move like that, especially a ten-year-old?

Maybe if I told my parents about it all–

There was a knock on my door then Mum entered the room. 'Peter.'

'Yeah?'

'Can I talk to you?'

'Okay,' I said apprehensively, still standing at the window.

'Don't worry, you're not in trouble.' She sat on my bed. 'Sit down,' She patted the vacant space.

I silently obliged.

'So, I just got off the phone with Jacob's mum,' I became nervous, 'she says you two are having trouble with some boys.' Her voice was light and soothing. 'Is this the same boy that was suspended?'

I looked away.

'Peter!' Her voice was now stern.

'Yeah, yeah it is.'

'Why didn't you tell us?'

'Because last time it made things worse. Jonesy is a fucking animal!'

'Peter!' she exclaimed, then immediately sighed and said, 'Jacob's mum told me everything: his accident, the bike being destroyed. Your dad and I felt bad for giving you a row–'

'You haven't told Dad, have you?'

'He's at work, but I'm going to have to. And we're going to have to sort this out once and for all. Jacob's mum and I are going to meet up to talk about it all – see what we can do. This can't go on any longer. It needs to stop. I'm not going to have my son be victimised.' She stood up. 'In the meantime if you're going out to play I suggest you do it where we can see you.'

'But, Mum– '

She held her hand up, 'No buts, Peter. Jacob's already been hurt. I don't want the same thing to happen to you. Understand?'

'Yes,' I mumbled.

'Understand?'

'Yes!'

'Good. Now you can help me with the housework.'

I hummed and hawed. Great. The last two weeks of summer and I was confined to help with housework and stay within eyesight as I played outside in the garden. And it was all because of Jonesy. It wasn't fair.

## 6

Jacob

The two weeks were now up, and I can honestly say it felt like a

countdown. Our parents tried their best to solve our issue: bully

helplines, talking to parents and, after school reopened, talk to the

teachers. I suppose there was one good thing: Pete and I got the day

off as our parents and the school advised we stay home so they

could reach some kind of compromise. I was over at Pete's house,

accompanied with a babysitter. Her name was Jenny, a good friend

of Pete's mum. She was cool. She made us hot chocolate with

marshmallows, and we got to watch a horror movie, John Car-

penter's The Thing.

Though we had fun watching films and playing board games

with Jenny, both of us were on edge. I felt as though it was parents'

night. We were expecting them to come home with furious rage

saying, 'You're slacking at school! You've lost jotters! You're not

paying attention!', and so forth. But that was simply not the case.

After they'd returned, they'd said their farewells to Jenny

and thanked her for looking after us. Then they sat us down in

Pete's living room. The T.V. was off, lamps were on, and the atmosphere, for Pete and I, was foreboding. *Why do we have to feel guilty? We haven't done anything wrong.*

I sat between Mum and Dad, and Pete his, Mike and Margaret. Mike was the first to speak. 'Well, we spoke to your headmaster. He said for you two to take notes whenever John or Jonesy, whatever you call him, does anything to you.'

Mum was next to speak. 'The school is going to notify their parents too, and arrange a meeting with them. But if anything happens, like what Mike said, take notes: time and date, and tell a teacher or us.'

Dad gave out a sigh.

'Robert, something you want to say?' Margaret asked.

'This – all of this, will not work. It's hopeless.'

Mum's frustration kicked in, 'Robert!'

Pete's parents were confused by this outburst.

'Sorry,' Mum said. 'Robert was bullied when he was younger. He thinks this won't be solved by democracy.'

'Oh? How did you solve it?' Margaret asked.

'You don't won't to know.'

'I think in a way we've all faced this crisis during our younger days,' Mike said. 'I was mostly picked on by my friends because they were bigger than me.'

'That's different. That's friends being friends. Getting hit and spat on, even having your head flushed down the toilet,' he referred to Pete, 'is a completely different story.'

'Robert!' Mum said again. 'That's enough.'

Mike and Margaret weren't happy at Dad's remark. Although, I did appreciate his honesty. Maybe all this was a waste of time.

As the adults talked and talked about our well-being, it was Pete's turn to talk, and I was surprised by his rash opinion. 'Shut up!' The room fell silent. Pete was on his feet. 'This isn't helping. Jacob and I are being bullied, and you're all just bickering. Jonesy will never stop; we either have to live with that or learn how to defend ourselves. It seems like the only way.'

'Violence isn't the answer, son,' Mike said.

'Then what is, Dad? Tell me cos I don't know anymore.' He started to sob then ran off towards his room, ending with a door being slammed.

I wanted to see if Pete was alright, but thought better of it. The adults were quiet for a moment, contemplating what was said during the little meeting.

Margaret broke the silence. 'Well, I can say it's been a long day for all of us. Think it's best to call it a night.'

Everyone nodded in agreement. As they said their goodbyes at the door, they mentioned their plans to take things further if our situation became worse: research, speaking to other parents who'd had their child victimised by the world of bullying, and the like. They said they would try all possible anti-bully helplines and, hopefully, find a solution.

## 7

As the years went by, my body took on an odd physical appearance as I reached the end of my sixth year at high-school. But Jonesy also took on a transformation. He was well-toned, and his attire was unorthodox to say the least: black jeans, leather jacket and dark hair. His demeanour was intimidating; anyone smaller and weaker than him would give him the opportunity to hassle them or instigate a fight. After what Pete and I went through throughout the years, he was still his usual menacing self. Nothing changed, even after talks with parents and teachers. It seemed as though experts didn't have a clue either, 'Talk to your antagonist. Ask them why they're hassling you. Get to the core of their feelings'.

What a lot of shit.

As for myself, my strength was considerably increased and the shape of my body moulded itself into a toned vigorous state. I didn't succumb to smoking or drugs of any sort unlike most adolescent teens going through their teenage years. My diet was reasonably healthy – nothing out of the ordinary, but there were times when I found it unusual my body became the way it was even though I didn't workout intensely (though I squeezed in a few hours of weight training) or have a strict diet.

I started to take an interest in running until I would run any chance I got especially from my house to the bus stop before and after high school. I hated getting the bus, in case Jonesy might make an appearance. High school was in Perth which was about twenty miles from where I lived. Jonesy on the other hand stayed in a small neighbourhood that was within walking distance to the school, but if he was in a lazy mood he would catch the bus. When this did happen I tried to remain incognito like sitting at the back and keeping my head down. Sometimes he would see me; other times he wouldn't. One time when he spotted me getting ready to depart with my bag over one shoulder, he stuck his foot out. I went tumbling to the floor and everyone on the bus laughed. Jonesy didn't, he just sat there with a smirk on his face, 'How was your trip?'

I stood up and carried on with my business.

He was much easier to avoid when I was at primary school. Almost everyday I would stay behind until his bus left then I would feel more at ease as I walked home.

The bus stop was a little way from my house, but the strange thing was, after the run was over, my body barely broke a sweat. Aren't most people prone to be out of breath after a long run?

There was always that uneasy feeling during my time at high school, but the running made me feel invincible. I felt in control. I felt free. I didn't attempt to make any friends except for Pete. I was more interested in keeping my head down and taking in as much knowledge as I could.

Others, however, were not so eager to learn – especially during biology. Two annoying twins, Frank and Jesse, sat in front of me.

*Why couldn't I get rid of these guys?*

They giggled and whispered to one another; what they were giggling about I couldn't tell, but I could only assume it was about me due to their quick glances in my direction. At the same time this was happening, the teacher was speaking to the class about biology and its fundamentals. She was becoming frustrated as the twins couldn't follow simple rudimentary instructions. She tried to continue but stopped abruptly and gave the two gigglers a piece of her mind. 'Frank and Jesse. Stop messing around and pay attention!'

'Sorry, Mrs Stevens,' one of them said, sarcastically.

I'd always found biology fascinating, but my concentration was distracted by the two gigglers in front of me.

After the small kerfuffle, Mrs Stevens continued. 'Now, who can tell me what metamorphosis means?' She looked around the room, waiting on an answer from the students but none were too eager until I put my hand up. 'Yes, Jacob?' she said.

'The process of transformation?'

'Good, Jacob. Metamorphosis is the change-of-form of a thing into a completely different one, typically an insect.'

'Geek,' one of the twins said under his breath.

Mrs Stevens gave them an intimidating look before she continued. 'Okay, class, I'm going to show you a short film that's based metamorphosis.' She hooked up the projector, turned the lights off and an image appeared on the wall. It was a silent, short film that depicted a caterpillar coating itself in a cocoon in different stages. It hatched during the final stage and exposed itself as a beautiful butterfly. As I sat there engrossed, my trance was disturbed by the school bell. Lunch time.

We all gathered our textbooks and other belongings as the teacher spoke about what to study for homework. Just as I was about to leave the room, one of the twins shoved into me, 'Watch where you're going, geek.' I said nothing and walked away.

My stomach rumbled from the smell of food as I entered the canteen and became worse while I waited in the queue.

Finally, I was served. I sat down near the window and dug into my fish fingers and chips at the same time as I read through some notes from my textbooks. I'd been sitting on my own for a while when I realised Pete was nowhere to be seen. We usually met up during the lunch hour. I waited a bit longer, but there was still no sign of him. *Maybe he's caught up in something.*

I pushed it out of my mind and went back to my studying and ate my food.

My eyes darted through the words of the textbook, but the letters started to blur. My body froze with fear as my brain registered that something was wrong. I stopped chewing and my fork fell, clattering onto the plate.

I couldn't see! My eyesight was completely gone. And my ears! They were suddenly sensitive to the slightest sounds, and the canteen wasn't exactly the quietest of all places. But I could hear everything: voices reverberating around the room, the sound of footfalls walking back and forth, not to mention chairs being scraped along the ground, was unbearable. Dishes being clanked together from being used and washed felt like glass shards penetrating my eardrums. There were other indistinct sounds, but they were all combined together making it hard to distinguish what they were.

As my senses were becoming distorted, the sensation I was experiencing finally reached its zenith and eventually came to a halt. My sight came into focus again, but it seemed different. It was still blurry, then it adjusted itself like a pair of binoculars until I saw things crystal clear. Everything was extremely distinct.

I was afraid to move my eyes in case I lost my sight again. I tested them by looking around the canteen. It all seemed sharp, but something was different. I focused on the wall opposite, just under a window. I appeared to have the ability to focus on every intricate detail of this wall. I saw the tiniest cracks embedded within the paintwork and the dirt and its texture that formed on the glass.

I was able to make out the seams of the students' clothes. I saw, clear as day, the pores of their skin and smelled the sweat and breath emanating from some of their bodies which wasn't particularly pleasant.

My hearing was also altered. My attention turned to some students at one of the adjacent tables. Their voices were loud which forced me to put my hands against my ears in an attempt to eradicate the din. I could hear their chewing as the food slowly disintegrated in their mouths and the grotesque swallowing sound that came after made my stomach churn.

A fly passed by in the distance and the whirr of its wings irritated me. I turned and saw its freakish body through close scrutiny.

I was able to see everything, hear everything and smell every vial and pleasant smell there was in the room. A gorgeous blonde prefect went by. I could smell the perfume on her as she walked past holding textbooks under one arm and licking, what looked like, and smelled like, a strawberry ice-cream. I could smell table sauces; vegetable soup that was being made; different spices; the fat that coated the pans.

The different mixtures of smells was becoming unbearable. Obviously others couldn't smell or see how I did. It made me feel uncomfortable seeing other students doing their social activities while I sat there with my hands against my ears looking frightened. It felt as though I was seeing it all through a microscope. My hearing was increasingly amplified as though I was listening through a parabolic microphone with the sound turned up to the max.

I wanted to scream but I would look stranger than I already was. So I tried to fight it – tried to withstand it.


Pete

Lunch had started! This was my opportunity to fit in some additional learning. The library was quiet – as usual. Many of the students were either filling their stomachs or finding a discreet location to fill their lungs with smoke. Not me. I had my head down in a book of physics embracing the smell of old and new books without realising the time.

I looked up at the clock. Twelve-thirty. *Shit! I was supposed to meet Jacob in the canteen.* Has it been half an hour?

I closed books and jotters, put them in my back and rushed out the door while being clumsily loud.

I rushed past students, sometimes bumping into them, nearly losing my glasses while listening to my stomach call out for food.

As soon as I knew it, I was on the floor. My glasses slipped from my head. I tried to focus and find them with a hand that did not succeed. And then, CRUNCH. I could hear manic laughter, and I knew the voice that spoke. There was a foot on top of my glasses that was attached to a blurry face that was Jonesy. 'What's the matter, Peter Pan, you lost your glasses?'

This was my new nickname they'd created for me.

'Frank, Jesse,' Jonesy commanded.

I felt arms take hold of me. I tried to shake them off but the twins were too strong. I was being dragged. I didn't know where they were taking me nor did I know if anyone was seeing this take place. I was dragged into a room that felt damp; there was a smell of urine and faeces mixed with deodorizing blocks.

As the twins held me, Paul seemed overenthusiastic about my suffering. He was enjoying Jonesy's antics as he shouted out with glee like he was at a party.

I could barely see but I knew it was Jonesy that stood in front of me. I could smell his leather mixed with his breath. 'Peter Pan had an accident. He lost his glasses. What do we do?'

'Eh, I think he needs a good wash,' Jesse said.

'What do you think, Peter Pan? Do you require a wash?'

'Jonesy, please!'

He made a sound of a buzzer going off and he spoke like a host from Family Fortunes. 'Wrong! The vote is unanimous.' A fist clashed against my stomach. My body slouched as I tried to catch my breath. I heard one of the cubicle doors being pushed open. 'Hurry up, get him in here,' Jonesy said.

I knew what was going to happen – history repeats itself!

I managed to work up the courage to fight back. It was hard to breathe, but I couldn't let this happen to me again. My legs flailed in the air and my left foot landed on what I think was Jonesy's face which escalated his frustration.

I continued to kick my legs until they were against the cubicle frame, they were parallel with the floor, causing the twins to push even harder. Jonesy then stepped in and took hold of them until our bodies were inside the cubicle. It was awkward considering the small, confined space which was a kind of advantage for me. But then I felt my hair being pulled which was a distraction and established an advantage for my assailants. My body shifted into an incline – head downwards.

I screamed as my head was pushed towards the toilet bowl. Lower and lower and lower…

## 8

Jacob

My clothes stuck to my body as sweat protruded from my skin. I was burning up. Perhaps I had some sort of fever, but then I was struck with heavy palpitations. My hand found my chest and I felt my heart pumping at an increasingly alarming rate. While holding one hand to my chest and the other against my ear, wishing I had more hands to cover the other ear, I heard a faint familiar sound through the loud murmuring voices.

Before I knew it, I was up on my feet, knocking my chair over from the sudden outburst. I continued to hold my ears as I reached the exit. Students gave me funny looks as I stumbled into them and bumped into chairs and tables. Some laughed and others sympathized as they witnessed my paroxysm.

I finally made it to the hallway and the canteen door closed behind me, blocking out some of the sounds. My back against a wall, I took a moment to steady myself, trying to take deep breaths and see if I could control whatever this was that was happening to me. The breathing helped but only a little; my chest wasn't heaving as much and the perspiring started to subside.

My eyesight didn't seem to be such a big issue; perhaps I was beginning to adjust to it. As for the hearing, it was still the same: loud and deafening. But now I could make out the faint sound I'd heard before.

It was a familiar voice and it was coming from the toilets – it was Pete! His voice was clear and perfectly audible. 'No. Please stop!' All that followed after his plea was a bubbling sound, then a muffled voice followed by laughter.

The toilets were down the hall and to my right; it seemed to take me forever to get there due to my condition, but knowing I had to help a friend in need motivated me. I weaved from side-to-side using the walls to regain my balance as I made my way drunkenly to the toilets.

At last! I made it to the gents and clumsily barged through the door and found Paul and Frank standing at the cubicle doorway. The side of the cubicle faced the door and Jesse was halfway inside, he was holding Pete's legs, and I knew who was doing the flushing.

Their laughter stopped after I'd entered.

Paul was first to notice me, 'Well, look who–'

I immediately charged towards him, took hold of his shirt and threw him into the mirror above the toilet sinks. The mirror smashed into pieces, scattering shards of glass to the floor.

A fist came in contact with my face. I stumbled back and saw Frank and Jesse charge at me. Jesse's fist clenched and threw a punch. I parried and gave him a right hook to the side of his face and felt his teeth clamp together from the impact. He fell clumsily next to Paul.

Frank tried to get a hit on me, but I swiftly moved in towards him, took hold of his shirt and shoved him against the wall. He was dazed and slid down to the floor.

It all happened so quickly. I didn't think I had the strength in me to perform these kinds of actions, but my fists were clenched, my chest heaved as adrenaline pumped its way through my body and I was fuelled with rage. I felt ready for anything.

I looked down at the three stunned bodies at my feet, but I knew there was still one more person to face. I turned and faced Jonesy, chest heaving in and out. 'COME ON!'

He was still standing in the cubicle. Pete was behind him on his knees, distraught and wet with toilet water.

Jonesy didn't say anything. An expression of anger filled his face as he gazed over at his incapacitated cronies, yet he still seemed keen to deal with me even though he was on his own.

He reached down into his pocket and pulled out a Swiss Army Knife, flicking it and grinning when a small blade appeared from its interior. He pointed it at me, 'You're dead. You're DEAD.'

He charged towards me. Our bodies clashed against the sink, his slightly taller form leaning over me, intimidating me. The hand with the knife was raised; he tried to bring it down onto my head, but I raised my left arm in defence. He was surprisingly strong and clearly determined to stab me. The force of his body pressed against mine, causing me to arch backwards against the sinks. Broken remnants of glass that still hung on the wall were only inches away from the back of my head. The blade was creeping closer to my eye and my whole body clenched as it continued towards my cheek bone.

The unknown strength I'd previously experienced surged through me once more. The blade started to move away from view.

A look of dissatisfaction formed on his face as my left hand took hold of his wrist. He tried to resist, but I was too strong for him. My hand twisted his wrist, squeezing it as I bent it round so far that a loud popping noise filled the air. Jonesy screamed in excruciating pain, and the knife dropped to the floor.

My right hand found his shirt and clenched at his clothing; it was drenched in sweat. I still held his right arm and pushed. We both crashed through a closed cubicle, destroying the door in the process. Jonesy lay still on the floor; lucky for me, he'd cushioned my fall.

I stood up and took a moment to breathe to calm my nerves. My senses seemed to be functioning normally again and I felt a sense of serenity now that it was over.

Pete was sitting against the cubicle wall with his hands to his face. 'Pete,' I said, 'are you all right?'

He didn't say anything. He wiped his face and nose with his sleeve, 'Fuck, Jacob. I tried to fight back,' he snorted, 'don't you dare tell anyone about this!'

'I won't. Let's go before they wake up.'

We left the cubicle, but before we did, Pete kicked Jonesy a few times in the leg with anger and frustration as the others were starting to stir.

Just then, another student walked in. His face formed an expression of disbelief and he stood there with his mouth open. 'Um… I'll find another toilet,' he said and hurried out. Pete and I followed a few moments later.

'We might get into trouble about this,' Pete said.

'Doesn't matter, I'll just tell them the truth. We should be fine.'

Pete kept glancing at me. I knew that look; it was one of analysation and scrutiny. 'Jacob,' he sighed, 'do you take drugs, like steroids or something?'

'What. No, God no! Why'd you ask that?'

'I saw the way you handled yourself; no one can possess that kind of strength, especially a boy of your stature. I know you work out sometimes, but that…'

I couldn't explain it myself. I told him I ran a lot, but that still didn't explain this strange strength I possessed. He still studied me, 'Stop staring, Pete.'

'I'm sorry, it's just you've changed through the years. I don't know what it is, but there's something odd about you.' Pete was concerned and in a way I too felt the same about my behaviour.

I didn't know what had just happened but whatever it was, it felt good: I felt strong, powerful, indestructible. After our conversation, we went back to class, but this wasn't going to pass unnoticed.

## 9

The bell rang to indicate school was over for another day but not for me. I put my bag over my shoulder and just as I left the classroom the headmistress, Miss Clark approached me. She held a couple of textbooks in one arm and her black-framed glasses matched her short hair. Her eyes were full of disappointment. 'Jacob, can I see you for a moment?'

'Yes, Miss Clark.'

I followed her without saying a word. I felt apprehensive as we walked towards her office. I knew what this was about and I knew I would have to face the outcome eventually.

Her office was small but somehow managed to fit in all the student documentation and other necessary files that were essential to the school. They were stored away in an orderly fashion inside steel drawers that were at the left of her desk. On the right, which I wasn't surprised to see, were Paul and the twins, sitting there on Miss Clark's comfortable couch. Jonesy's injuries must've been too severe considering he wasn't present. Their eyes regarded me as I walked in.

Pete was also present. He seemed cleaner than before with the help from the school nurse. He sat on one of the chairs facing Miss Clark's desk – feeling lost without his glasses – with his head down, picking at his nails. No doubt an act of nervousness. There was also another person there; it was the student who'd come into the toilets after the confrontation. I guessed he'd reported the incident, but I didn't blame him. Maybe his complaining about the incident would motivate Miss Clark to do something about Jonesy.

My assailants were pretty beaten up. It looked as though Paul had suffered lacerations on one side of his face and most likely on his back considering it came in contact with the glass mirror. Frank seemed to be in good form; his injuries weren't visible, but I supposed the shove I gave him had left him with severe muscle pains about the neck and back. Jesse's facial features were starting to change in a non-recognisable state. Only one of his eyes was directed towards me because his other was severely swollen to the stage that it was basically closed, purple and black bruising starting to colour the skin. As I stared at their injuries a small smile broke out on my face.

'Something funny, Jacob?' Miss Clark asked sternly as she sat at her desk.

'No, Miss Clark,' I said, trying to devoid myself of my humorous state.

'Well, let me assure you that this is no laughing matter, Jacob. Just look at the state of them...' she indicated to the three ailing students on the couch, '...and not to mention John, who is in hospital with a sprained wrist. Just what exactly happened?'

I looked at Pete considering he was the victim in all of this. 'Pete, do you want to tell her?'

Miss Clark's hands interlaced and she rested her elbows on her desk waiting for an explanation. 'Peter?'

'Um... I...'

I decided to help him, 'Those assholes shoved his head down the toilet.'

'Peter can talk for himself, Jacob, and mind your language!' She turned her attention back towards Pete again. 'Peter, is this true?'

He managed to achieve a bit of confidence and spoke, 'Yes, Miss.'

'Wimp,' came a voice from the couch.

Miss Clark's head snapped towards that direction, 'Enough!'

I continued, 'I was in the canteen and I rushed in after I heard what was happening to Pete and then—'

'Wait,' she interrupted, 'you heard that?'

'Yeah.'

'You must have extraordinarily good hearing,' she said, sceptically.

'Eh, I guess I was at the right place at the right time,' I chuckled.

She motioned me to continue. 'After I walked in, these three,' I pointed to Paul and the twins, 'came at me and then Jonesy pulled a knife on me. It was self-defence.'

Miss Clark took her glasses off, clearly frustrated and rubbed the bridge of her nose. She looked at Paul and the twins, her voice sincere, 'Is this true? Did John have a knife?'

'No, Miss,' Frank said.

'You fucking liars.'

'JACOB!' Miss Clark shouted.

I lowered my head. 'Sorry, Miss,' I said sheepishly.

She was quiet for a moment, put her glasses back on then spoke. 'Regardless of who's telling the truth or not, this kind of behaviour is unacceptable and will *not* be tolerated. Do you understand?'

I tried to reason with her, 'But they—'

She put her hand up to block my words, 'Do you understand?'

I suppressed my emotions. 'Yes, Miss Clark.'

'I swear to you this will not go unnoticed. School property has been severely damaged and students are now apparently carrying concealed weapons throughout the building.'

She turned her gaze towards the three students on the couch with their heads down. 'We carry out a strict policy here at the school to provide a safe environment for all students. Unfortunately, the police will have to be involved. So an investigation will take place and when it's complete, someone is looking at immediate expulsion.'

Innocent or not, my heart sank when she said "expulsion" and I knew Pete felt the same. It was self-defence on my part, but what was I supposed to have done? Let them continue flushing Pete's head down the toilet? Let Jonesy stab me with his knife? Ultimately, Pete was the victim; he was the innocent one out of the lot of us and Miss Clark should know that. She was aware of our situation; after all, it had been happening throughout the years, but it seemed as though Pete and I were reliving our childhood once more. History was repeating itself, and no one, still, was doing anything about it.

Miss Clark's gaze shifted behind me to look at the student who'd reported us.

I turned to him. He was a freckled-faced ginger haired boy that was in a year below me. He was standing there obviously feeling awkward, scratching his hair and fiddling with his pockets. Miss Clark must've forgotten he was there. 'Sorry, Harry. You can go now.'

'Thanks, Miss Clark,' he said and quickly left the room.

Miss Clark continued, 'This is getting ridiculous. I know you all don't get along, but you're nearing the end of school and soon you'll have jobs. Why do you persist on hassling each other?'

'Ask them that,' I said.

'Jacob!' She stared at me through her black-framed glasses then took a moment to breathe. 'I suggest you all go home and have a good think about what has occurred today and maybe you'll see sense. Jacob, Peter, you two leave first, then you three,' she pointed to the boys on the couch. 'God forbid, I don't want anymore malicious behaviour while exiting the school. You're all free to go,' she said while sorting out paperwork on her desk.

It was a quiet exit as we all left her office. Pete and I were first to leave then Paul and the twins a few moments later. Pete spoke about the whole affair, but I didn't listen. I came up with an idea in my head as we stepped outside.

I turned around to face the three injured boys that were standing at the top of the stairs. 'Look, Miss Clark is right, why don't we settle this? We've nearly finished school and we'll be moving on with our lives so what's the point in fighting?'

They didn't answer. They were silent.

I stuck out my hand, hoping it would make contact with one of theirs and end all this with a simple handshake. 'What do you say… friends?'

It was Jesse that approached. His steps were slow as he moved down the stairs. He eyed my hand as if he'd never seen one before. His right hand started to rise and was close to coming in contact with mine, but he swiftly slapped it away and shoved me out the way. Paul and Frank followed. 'Fuck you,' was the reply I got.

My hand lowered disappointedly. 'You tried,' Pete said as he patted me on the back. 'But it's pointless. Why bother? I guess sometimes people never change.'

'I know. I thought I'd try.'

## 10

The day seemed to drag on forever; it felt as though it was one problem after the other. Pete and I managed to catch the late bus, but we were weary. We just wanted to get home. The school had already been in contact with our parents to let them know what had happened making us both anxious.

I wasn't really concerned about what I'd done; basically, a good friend of mine was in distress and I acted immediately so, technically, I'd done nothing wrong – it was self-defence.

The bus approached Newburgh from Perth and it stopped at the top of town. It was quite a walk to my house, but I thought I'd join Pete; he seemed lost without his glasses. He was still unsettled, his face full of worry.

We stepped off the bus and he blurted out, 'Shit, Jacob, what am I going to say to my mum and dad? I can't face them.'

'Relax. You're the victim here, remember? You've done nothing wrong. It's those other assholes. Besides, they know about the whole Jonesy thing. They tried years ago, but didn't get any-where.'

'What're you saying?'

'I'm saying, we might have to deal with this ourselves. Jonesy had a knife today so there's no telling how far he might go.'

'I'm so sick of their shit. We say something about it and fuck all gets done. It's like people are just turning a blind eye.' Pete's hands were clenched and his voice emotional.

We got to his house, and he said he would manage the rest of the way. 'Remember, Pete, you've done nothing wrong. Just tell the truth and you'll be fine,' I said calmly.

He took a breath, 'Okay, I'll tell them and we'll see what happens tomorrow, but we should watch our backs because we haven't heard the last of them considering what happened today.'

I paused and gave it a thought. I knew we hadn't heard the last of them, and when Jonesy got out of hospital it was going to be hell. From here on it was going to be worse, and I now knew what he was capable of. 'I know,' I said. 'I'll see you tomorrow.' I took off while watching Pete feel his way to the front door. He eventually found the handle and entered.

Dusk started to envelope the town and dark bruised-looking clouds hovered above the earth like misshapen blips. As I made my way home, a strange feeling came over me like I was being watched. There were people coming to and fro, but it felt like eyes were scrutinising my every move. I guessed the events of the past few hours had affected my mind or maybe I was just being paranoid.

I shrugged it off and kept walking towards the road that cut off from the high street and into the quiet bungalows near my house. I tried to shake off the feeling, but my instincts were telling me something wasn't right.

I turned and looked at my surroundings; everything seemed normal: certain individuals going about their day-to-day lives; the odd car going by to reach its specific destination, but then my eyes fell on a vehicle – a black BMW with tinted windows. It was parked a few yards up from the corner I was about to take. I focused my gaze and tried to get a view of the driver but couldn't. I didn't want to arouse suspicion so I averted my eyes and continued my journey down the road.

I caught the vehicle's lights in my peripheral vision just before I was out of sight. I hoped they would pass and continue going straight on, but they turned the corner onto the same road.

I could sense the vehicle behind me, its tyres slowly rolling forward, its exhaust emitting small revs. I picked up my pace; the car did the same. There was no doubt about it – I was being followed, but what did they want? I was thinking of approaching the car and demanding an explanation. It was probably someone being foolish and playing a trick on me or so I hoped.

As the thought of speaking to the driver ran through my mind, I turned my head towards the car. The full beam of its lights blinded me and it started to speed up. 'Oh shit!' I exclaimed as I broke into a sprint.

The car's bright lights felt like eyes boring into my back. The vehicle was right behind me now, like a phantom chasing me down. I needed a plan and I had to think fast otherwise I was going to be roadkill. I swerved left and right, but it followed. I wasn't going to lose them; the road was too open and I was too exposed. My only option was to cut through the gardens of the houses.

I swiftly moved to the left and in the direction of the houses to try and elude my tormentors. I hurdle-jumped the small fence and gave a quick glance behind me. The vehicle stopped for a second then hurtled forward with a screech of tyres, probably to cut me off on the other side of the houses.

I flew out the receiving end of the gardens, hoping they didn't know Newburgh as well as I did. Basically, my neighbourhood was something of a maze; there were small pathways that intertwined with one another. It made a pleasant peaceful walk, but today it also provided me with plenty of hiding spots.

As I quickly crossed the street to enter the maze, I caught sight of the vehicle up ahead in the distance. It was reversing and heading in my direction. I moved inside the maze and hugged a wall hoping the driver hadn't seen me. I peeked out and felt the vehicle's vibration and smelled its fumes. Then it was in my line of sight. I ducked back. It crept past as I watched through a small gap in the maze.

After it passed, I stayed in the shadows awhile, my breathing loud in my ears. An involuntary shiver shot through me. Thank goodness they'd gone.

It seemed as though I was in the clear. I set off for home but not without thinking about what had just occurred. Darkness was now imminent and my parents were probably worried sick by now.

The pathway I was on led to a small quiet road and from there was home. I still didn't feel right and I couldn't help but wonder if the phantom-vehicle would be waiting for me.

The neighbourhood felt still; it was always quiet, but this time it was different. It was almost like I was in one of those western movies when the townsfolk flee as a duel is about to take place. I pictured myself as a gunslinger walking in the centre of town as people closed their windows and doors in a frightful panic from the gunslinger villain. Something inside was telling me the threat had not yet been neutralized.

My prediction was right. As my house came into view, there it was: the phantom-vehicle was sitting a few yards from my front door. Its dark paintwork almost camouflaged its entire body giving off an eerie effect.

I stopped in my tracks as the engine started up. I shrugged off my school-bag and threw it on the grass, assuming they didn't want the contents that were inside.

*I would collect it later.* If there was a later.

At first the vehicle just sat there, revving its engine like it was testing me. I could feel the driver's eyes on me and they probably felt mine. It was somewhat ironic considering I pictured a tumble-weed crossing our paths. The only plan I had was to run in the opposite direction; if I went home, they would know where I lived and I didn't want to put my family's lives in jeopardy. I had to lead them away, had to make them think I lived somewhere else. I turned right and cut through the grass that was surrounded by a small road that eventually led into the main road. I heard the vehicle's low mumble as it crept behind me.

My pace picked up as I turned the corner. I looked behind and the car followed. Then I stopped, a smile breaking out on my face. All the fear I'd felt fell away; it was my turn to toy with them now.

The car had slowed to a stop and I abruptly broke out into a sprint. Tyres screamed against tarmac as the wheels span and full-beam lights once again blinded my surroundings. I had to admit, if this vehicle wanted me dead it could've done it by now, so why was it tormenting me?

I ran as fast as I could; the psychological feeling of someone or something chasing you increases the speed of the runner which was exactly what was happening to me. My heart rate was accelerating, adrenaline coursing through my body. This feeling wasn't like the one I'd previously had in the canteen. This was different. However, I'd experienced this feeling before when I faced off against Jonesy on Pete's bike, only this time it wasn't a short burst of speed.

I was running the same speed as the vehicles passing me – it was a 30 zone. The odd person on the side-walk panicked and quickly moved aside, their curious eyes staring at me. I heard the quick succession of whooshing sounds from objects that I passed and felt my hair becoming tousled due to the wind and speed.

Once again, I felt powerful. Indestructible. And I felt… alive!

For a moment, I thought I had the upper hand. Up ahead was a large wooden fence attached to the side of a house in the distance. There was nowhere else to go; the road ended and fed into a small cul-de-sac area. I thought about my options: turn back and face my foes? Or continue on? I went with the latter.

My eyes focused on the fence in front of me. It had to be ten feet in height. I continued to run towards it. I could've gone through the cul-de-sac, but something drove me towards the fence.

I looked behind me to see where the phantom-vehicle was. It dodged parked cars and overtook others; it even went on the wrong side of the road just to catch up to me and it was getting closer.

Despite the fact this vehicle had a death wish, I still had the intention to interact with it, to communicate with the driver to see what they wanted, but my instincts were telling me otherwise. I don't know why I still went for the fence. After all, it was too big to jump and I wouldn't have any time to climb it. I was fucked either way.

My nerves were becoming jittery and I started to panic. It threatened to overwhelm me as the vehicle loomed closer, its engine roaring in my ears and the vibration of its revs pulsating through me. The pressure mounted as its lights acted like a powerful spotlight; all I could make out was the fence surrounded in darkness.

I thought about the authorities scraping my remains off the ground. I thought about Mum and Dad breaking down into tears and shock when they witnessed what was left of my body. But that wasn't going to happen! I wouldn't let it.

I ran up to the fence and simultaneously lifted one leg off the ground as the other pushed. Before I knew it, I was in mid-air!

I landed on my feet on the other side of the fence. I heard the vehicle's tyres protest as it squealed to a halt. It hit the fence, but thankfully it didn't come crashing through. I stumbled backwards and fell to the ground. I listened, dumbfounded as the vehicle pulled away and sped up the road.

I sat up against the fence to calm my nerves hoping that that was the end of the phantom-vehicle. I took a moment to gather my thoughts and studied the size of the fence. The stunt I had just performed was a clear-cut jump; no part of my body had touched the fence as I leapt. Was that possible? Furthermore, the jump had felt like a reflex, as if my body automatically knew it was in a life-threatening situation.

I was lost in thought until I realised the time. I peeked out from where I was just to make sure it was clear. There didn't seem to be any sign of them. There didn't even seem to be any sign of the people that occupied the house. Thank goodness.

crossing the streets and cutting through a couple of gardens I embraced my newfound ability by jumping fences. But it seemed they had given up too easily as I made my journey home. Why didn't they just ram through the fence? They seemed crazy enough to pull a stunt like that off.

Whoever that driver was, it seemed he or she had a problem with me, but why? Was it a member of Jonesy's family or a friend out for revenge? I'd better be more careful; it seemed I needed to watch my back at all times. It felt like I was facing problem after problem. I'd faced Jonesy in the toilets, I'd eluded the phantom-vehicle; now I had to face another problem… my parents. I made my way to my house but not before retrieving my school-bag first.

## 11

## Pete

After Jacob had left, I entered my house to witness two blurred out faces. 'Good God, Peter, where are your glasses?' Dad asked.

'Eh… I had an accident.'

I didn't have to see their expressions to know what they were thinking. 'Let me guess, Jonesy?' Mum was abrupt.

I nodded.

'What happened this time?' Anger was rising in Dad's voice.

'They attacked me and broke my glasses.'

'Ah, shit!'

'Mike, watch your language,' Mum said as Dad paced the living room.

'This has gone on too long. Those little shits!'

'Mike, calm down.'

I wanted to tell the rest of the story: the knife, my head being flushed and Jacob defending us both, but that would only fuel his rage; he could end up doing something he could regret.

Dad continued his rant, 'Why won't anyone do anything? Why–'

'The police might be involved.'

Dad stopped in his tracks.

'What?' Mum was puzzled.

'The police…' I stuttered, 'm…might be involved.'

'Why?' Dad asked.

'Jonesy threatened us with a knife.'

The two fell silent. Mum sat on the couch in disbelief, but Dad was staring at me intently. 'Knife?' he said quietly.

I nodded.

'Okay, okay. That's it.' He stormed out of the living room to the door, and grabbed his jacket that was hanging up.

'Mike, what are you doing?' Mum was now frightened by his behaviour.

'Something we should've done a long time ago. I'm going to visit his parents.'

'No! You'll only make things worse,' I said.

'Worse than it already is? It's one thing being name-called or hit a few times, but a knife…' Dad quickly put the jacket on, grabbed his car keys then pointed to me. 'You, you're coming with me.'

'What? No!' I panicked.

'Yes. It's times you started to defend yourself.'

He basically dragged me out the door while Mum protested this idea. 'Stop, don't do this.' But Dad didn't listen. He was too fuelled up. He coaxed me into the passenger seat, went round the front, climbed in and slammed the driver's door. The car took off with screeching tires.

Jacob

I went an alternate route in case the vehicle was still patrolling the neighbourhood. There didn't seem to be any sign of it; I guessed they were really gone and I had the all clear.

I had one last look around as I placed my hand on the front door to make sure I wasn't being watched. I jumped at the sound of the door snapping open to reveal a stark raving Mother. Her long dark hair was tousled as if she'd been unsettled and riddled with uncontrollable nerves from worry of my whereabouts.

'Where the hell have you been? We've been worried sick. Do you know what time it is?'

I looked over her shoulder at the clock hanging on the wall of the hallway. Near enough 6:30pm.

*Holy shit!* I guessed time eases its way out of focus and flies when your life is being tested.

Mum stood there, waiting on an explanation and she wasn't going to move till I gave it to her. I had to come up with an excuse; I wanted to tell her what happened but bit my tongue – I didn't want to worry her even more. I came up with the only excuse I had. Part truth and part lie. 'We got kept behind at school and afterwards I went to Pete's house. I'm sorry, Mum. He was–'

'Don't lie, Jacob. I've just came off the phone to Peter's Mum. Mike and Peter are going to Jonesy's house to see his parents. She told me everything: the knife, the police…'

*Shit!* I was caught by surprise.

Did Mike even know where they lived? 'I had to do something. Pete was in trouble, I acted.'

Dad was silent. Mum kneaded her temples. 'It's not your fault, Jacob. You were just defending yourself. This whole thing has been hell for all of us.'

'I know. But no one's helping us. I felt weird today at school, like something forced me to do what I did.'

Mum just changed the subject. 'Never mind that for now, Jacob.'

I didn't expect this kind of reply. I was dumbfounded and tried to think of why she didn't want to hear about the strange turn I had.

I stared at her in bafflement. She hastily directed me into the living room. Her movements were quick and clumsy like she was preparing for the apocalypse.

Dad was sitting on his recliner, still quiet. He seemed less troubled than Mum did – he was too busy gazing at the T.V. which depicted a BREAKING NEWS bulletin.

'Look,' Mum said, pointing at the screen. 'Haven't you heard?'

'Strange disappearances are still occurring throughout Perth…' a reporter said, standing outside a house which I assumed was owned by the occupants that had disappeared. 'There is no trace and no witnesses at this time, but if you see these people–' a screen came up with multiple individuals that had gone missing in the past month or so– 'please contact the police immediately.'

The news made no difference to me; people disappeared all the time, but it was kind of worrying considering Perth was only a twenty-minute drive.

Mum sensed I had the wrong attitude towards this situation; she was caring but a little too caring. 'This is serious, Jacob! Robert, tell him.'

'Listen to your mother, Jacob,' he said calmly.

'Geez, some help you are,' she said.

'Well, he is home, Helen. And I think you're watching too much of the news. You're taking it a bit too far.'

'But we have to be prepared; especially after that visit from that strange man, and why are you not worried about what Mike might do?'

'Because I told you a long time ago,' Dad stood up, 'everything we would try was going to be a waste of time, and now look, the police are involved and now we have kids with knives. I think Jacob did the right thing, and if you ask me so is Mike. You want to get rid of something, you're gonna have to cut the head off the snake.

'And don't dwell on the past, Helen.' Dad changed the subject to the stranger claiming to be my uncle. 'That man is probably long gone.'

Dad was now agitated. He was a relaxed man, but when the shit hit the fan, that would be his time to step in and when he went off on one, you couldn't stop him, like the performance he put on while confronting the stranger we had years ago. Although, it felt like he was also reliving his past but through my perspective. I think it was having a bad effect for him. How did he solve his issues during his childhood?

Mum turned her attention back to the T.V. and continued her talk about my well-being.

'What do you want me to do?' I asked.

'I want you to be responsible. You're near enough an adult now and irresponsibility can lead you to that,' she pointed towards the screen again. 'It could be your face up on those photos and your body could be in the boot of a car right now.'

I wished she hadn't said that, as harsh as it was, I knew she was almost accurate in what she'd said. I could've been in the boot of a car – a certain black BMW.

'Okay, okay. I'm fine and I'm sorry,' I admitted defeat.

She breathed out a sigh of relief, 'I'm just worried something might happen: the knife, the police, the news–'

'But nothing happened and I'm home. I'm fine. Stop worrying. Watching the news isn't healthy, Mum, and you overthink things.'

'I know, son, I know.' The subject was out the way and it immediately changed. 'I made you mince and tatties, but you'll need to heat it up in the microwave.'

Mum would usually have an outburst of rage and worry every time something unfortunate happened, whether it was a fight out on the street or a terrorist attack on the news. Whatever it was, she would react by applying an uncontrollable urge to protect her loved ones. The initial panic would last a certain amount of time before she became subdued, but her worries were always still tucked away somewhere deep in her mind.

Later, I sat there in the dining room digging into my mince and tatties. I seemed to be burning a lot of calories these days. Mum went for a lie down and Dad came into the kitchen. He sat on the chair next to me. 'Your mum is full of stress. I know her nagging can be a bit annoying, but this shit with the school and those boys has had a missive impact on her mind.'

'I know, but how do you think I feel, Dad. My whole life I've to look over my shoulder. Pete was being attacked and I intervened. What else could have I have done? You would've done the same thing, right?'

He was silent with his elbows on the table and his chin resting on his hands.

'You would've done the same thing, right, Dad?'

His eyes quickly turned towards me. It felt like I had hit a nerve – awoken something that had been buried for years.

I hesitated for a moment, 'Dad?'

He just sighed and waited, like he was working up the courage to tell me something. 'It takes a lot of balls to stand up to these things, and you've done just that. You also protected a friend as well. I'm going to tell you the opposite my dad told me: I'm proud of you, Jacob.'

'You are?'

'Your mum might think otherwise, but I know deep down she's proud of you too. Your methods might be unorthodox, but what the hell, no one else is doing anything.'

I had to ask about his past. 'What did you do – when you were bullied?'

I could see he was working the words in his head as it was lowered facing the table. It came up and his eyes reverted back to me. 'I was a skinny when I was about your age. I knew I wasn't the most attractive boy at school, but a certain other boy took offence to my appearance. He kept hassling me and hassling me. What was his name again?' he said to himself.

He clicked his fingers as though they would trigger a name. 'Billy! That was it. I can't remember his second name, but he was a pain in the arse. He beat me up countless times until I couldn't take any more. One time he broke my rib as he pinned me to the lockers. He threatened to stab me with pencils. He punched, kicked and spat. You name it, he did it all.'

'What did you do?'

'Well, throughout most of my school days I turned to a lot of Kung-Fu movies. I studied their moves – I even borrowed books on martial arts from the library.

'It took time. I knew I had to tolerate Billy's malicious behaviour until one day I managed to catch him while he was on his own. I faced him. I was shaking and scared as I clenched my fists. He saw my fists and knew I wanted to engage. A look of pure menace formed on his face with his hands also forming into fists. We both charged at one another. We scrapped and rolled to the ground until he was on top of me. A left and right hook came to my face; my lip bled and I felt and heard my nose crack. My knee came up and made contact with his groin. Billy gave out a scream, giving me a few seconds window to have the upper hand. I screamed with rage as I turned him over until I was the one on top of him. It's amazing what you can do when you're overcome with adrenaline. I punched his face with left and right hooks until it was black and blue and his nose was bleeding like there was no tomorrow. But I didn't stop; I couldn't. The frenzy in me was too strong. I screamed and roared like a savage beast.'

Dad lowered his head in disappointment.

'Dad?'

He abruptly continued. 'Billy was in hospital after that. There was a lot of stitches involved, but…' he paused, 'he was left with permanent brain damage. The police, my parents and Billy's went through hell; all because of me. I was institutionalised for young offenders, but got out early due to good behaviour.

'I wasn't proud when I was out.'

'What happened to Billy?'

'He lived out the rest of his school days with learning difficulties. He got all the support he needed. I don't know where he is now, but if I could see him, I would tell him I'm sorry. Sorry for what I'd done,' he said with a tremble in his bottom lip. I knew it wasn't easy for him to tell me this, but he did. And in a way I'm glad he did as I could've suffered the same situation as he did.

He was still silent as I continued to eat my food that was now cold. He stared into nothing. 'Thanks, Dad,' I broke his train of thought.

'For what?'

'For telling me. I know it wasn't easy for you to tell me that part of your life.'

He gave out a half smile. 'My point is, Jacob, if you are facing confrontation and you let that rage within you free, you can overcome any obstacle. But just be careful. Consequences always come from your actions. Don't make the same mistake I did, you understand?'

'Yeah.'

'Good,' he ruffled my hair as he stood up. 'Let's keep what I said to ourselves, okay?'

'Sure, Dad.'

'I'd rather not let your mother know.'

He was about to walk back to the living room when I stopped him in his tracks. 'Dad!'

'Yeah?'

'What about Pete and Mike?'

He gave it a thought. Should we've helped them confront Jonesy's parents? Were they just as violent as him? 'We'll ride it through for the night. I'll be expecting a phone call – maybe tonight – if not, tomorrow then see where we'll go from there.'

I nodded in agreement, and Dad went back to his recliner to watch T.V.

## 12

Pete

Dad sped through country roads until we arrived at a small town just outside Perth. He even went through red lights with clenched teeth and a white-knuckled tightness on the steering wheel. 'Dad, slow down!'

He did not answer.

I wasn't sure where we were, but Dad seemed to have a rough idea of where he was going. He spotted the house he was looking for, braked harshly and the car came to a halt half on pavement and road. He got out, leaving his door open and stropped towards the house that was a display of overgrown weeds combined with a squint rusty fence.

My vision wasn't very good; all I heard were sounds: a manic bang on the front door followed by shouts. 'Where's John!' Dad demanded.

'Who the fuck are you?' came a man's voice which I assumed was Jonesy's dad.

'I'm the one that's going to sort this out. Do you realise what your son is doing to mine? Do you? He's made his life a living hell.'

'How dare you come here and yell your head off,' came a woman's voice. 'Hank, call the police.'

'Yeah, you call them and tell them how your son threatened mine with a fucking knife. Where the hell is that little shit?'

I didn't tell Dad he was in hospital, besides I didn't think he'd listen.

Next was the sound of a fist making contact with someone else. I saw a blurred figure, which was obviously Dad, staggering. He fell a few feet back followed by Jonesy's dad. I could see them both scrapping in the garden. Arms flailed, and a few kicks partook in this malicious act.

I had to do something.

I got out the car and cautiously walked towards the garden as the grunting of the two fighters became more profound. I wasn't able to make out the woman that was probably Jonesy's mum, but I assumed she was phoning the police.

'Dad, stop it,' I pleaded as the two blurs became more focused as I got closer. There was no reasoning with them. They punched and kicked until eventually tumbling to the ground. I entered the garden and tried to break them up. Next thing I knew I felt a powerful throbbing on my cheek after a fist made contact with it. Jonesy's dad – Hank – was in a state of uncontrollable rage, but as soon as he realised he'd hit a ten-year-old, his rage dispersed.

Everything came to a halt. The two adults looked at me as they witnessed a boy nursing his face. Hank stood back with his hands up, 'Oh my God! I'm so sorry.'

'You fucking asshole!' Dad got up to attend to me.

'I'm sorry,' Hank continued. He walked back to his house.

Jonesy's mum was in a state of shock, 'Oh my God, Hank. What have you done?'

They both closed the door and locked it to prevent further assaults.

Dad coaxed me back to the car as my face throbbed. I sat on the passenger seat with the door open as Dad tried to comfort me. His constant apologies served no meaning as my pain overshadowed everything that was happening.

Soon after the police arrived. Dad's hands still caressed my face as he watched them pull up near Jonesy's house. 'I'm so sorry. This is all my fault. What have I done?' he sobbed.

I spent most of the night at the police station giving my statement; Dad did the same. We gave our story, and the amount of times we'd said it was becoming desensitizing. A kindly officer – Inspector Gregory – gave me an icepack for my face; it throbbed, and was turning black and blue as I sat there smelling nothing but coffee. Dad was held in custody for breach of the peace. He was allowed a phone call, and he seemed more afraid of phoning Mum than he did the fight.

Hank was arrested which probably made things worse for Jonesy. He was probably still in hospital recuperating after Jacob dealt with him. However, all this was going to make things ten-times worse. When Jonesy was completely healed he'd unleash his rampage, I know that for a fact. Thanks, Dad!

Half an hour later a concerned Mum walked in the station. She saw me sitting there with a half-melted icepack. She saw my face which caused tears to form and trail down her face. She rushed over to me and knelt down so that we were eye level. 'Peter,' her hand caressed my cheek. Her concern immediately changed to anger. 'Where's your dad?' she said behind clenched teeth. Just then Dad showed up. Mum stood, walked over to him and started to throw punches and slaps. Dad didn't say anything, he just had to take it. The staff at the station had a quick glance then went back to their duties; I think they'd seen this kind of behaviour before.

I stood up and intervened the beating, 'Mum, MUM!'

She stopped and turned her attention to me. 'Look, Peter, look at your face.' Her attention turned towards the police officer that escorted Dad from the cells. 'Where is he? Where's the man that hurt my son?'

'Ma'am, you need to calm down–' Gregory tried to explain.

'Don't tell me to calm down. Look at his face, for Christ's sake!'

'Margaret, please.' Dad tried to calm her by placing a hand on her shoulder. She quickly shoved it off.

'Don't touch me,' her voice trembled and tears of rage continued to roll down her cheeks as she gazed at Dad.

The Inspector spoke between them to break the tension. 'The man that hit your son has been charged. Your husband on the other hand knows he done something foolish. Giving the lack of seriousness, he's been cautioned. We'll follow through with your husband and son's statement about the attack towards him. But just remember, it may have been instigated.'

'What?' Mum's head snapped towards the Inspector.

He put his hands up in defeat, 'All I'm saying is that your husband went to the house to pick a fight.'

'So you're telling me you're not going to do anything about my son being attacked?'

Gregory didn't answer her. His hands were tied.

Mum looked around at the other staff going to and fro with their business. Disgust and disappointment formed on her face until Gregory came round from his desk. 'Look, whatever issues you have, I suggest you go home and try to talk them over. I really want to help, but the law's the law.'

She glared at the Inspector and said, 'Peter, we're going home.' She stormed out and I followed her with Dad further behind, but I had a quick glance back toward the Inspector. He just lowered

his head and looked as if he was disappointed with himself.

## 13

Jacob

The night was late and a heavy wind whistled against the house which made it difficult for me to fall asleep. I tossed and turned, but my mind was racing with thoughts I couldn't dissipate. The feeling of foreboding was profound; images of the vehicle that stalked me cycled through my mind. I imagined different outcomes: what if I had spoken to the driver and what if I wasn't lying in my bed safe and sound and my body was on the ground with my entrails hanging out? All kinds of outcomes were playing in my head. Why were they following me? If it was a joke, it wasn't very funny.

Eventually, my mind was at ease and I drifted off into a deep slumber. But, just like reality, I was faced with other forces, this time of the dream world. It was a recurring dream I'd had for years. But as it progressed, it started to feel real and my emotions intertwined between the real world and the dream world; my senses were heightened too. Was I achieving a kind of lucidity within the dream?

It started off with me fleeing from an unknown foe. But instead of having the feeling of fear I usually experienced when I had this dream, a strange euphoria took over. This euphoria surged through my body as I ran from the monstrosity, but why wasn't I afraid this time?

I kept running but worked up the courage to look behind me... there was nothing – no monster of any kind – only an inky-black oblivion.

Where was it?

As the dream further progressed, I was able to make out something in the distance. It appeared to be a distinct shape. I moved towards this shape and, as I got closer, I could make out a light in front of it which caused a silhouette effect. The more steps I took, the more vivid the shape became. I could now clearly see it was a young man; he was hysterical and running like he was afraid of something. Afraid of what?

The runner seemed helpless; he was naked and I could hear his rapid breathing as his heart pounded and I could smell his sweat; his back was glistening with it. His heartbeat was becoming faster and faster as an uncontrollable force was driving me towards him.

Suddenly, when I was only a few inches from his back, he turned around, exposing his face. His eyes met mine, his frightened face in full view. My mind immediately registered that it was me – I was looking at myself.

Even though I realised the runner was me, I kept pursuing him like I was hunting him down. That's when I realised *I* was performing the actions of the monster that had chased me in my dreams since I'd been an infant. My other self raised a hand as if trying to fend off an attack.

And then it happened. It was all so quick, I could only make out snippets. There was a hand, covered in light-brown fur, with claws instead of fingers. The neck of my human self was exposed and I heard a snarl before blood spilled as teeth came into contact with skin. Then I woke up.

## 14

I looked around, my eyes falling on my bedside clock: just after 3am. My sheet was drenched from sweat and my heart rate was slowly calming down. I threw back the covers and sat on the edge of the bed. My vision was blurred; in fact, everything felt distorted as I battled to adjust to the real world.

I got up, went through to the bathroom and stood at the mirror. I hesitated to turn the light on in case my reflection might be something else. I turned it on… No monster. It was just me. My hair was a mess and my eyes were weary. I cupped my hands under the cold water and splashed it over my face. Despite the shocking chill of the water, the dream-daze still lingered – that feeling of waking from something so vivid yet the subconscious was still bound.

I went back to bed, but all I did was stare at the ceiling. My mind couldn't shut off and there was no chance of sleep.

The shrill song of the birds in the trees outside came to my ears and daylight started to creep in through my curtains. Morning.

Perhaps I'd dozed off after all. I tugged the covers over my head as I tried to fit in a snooze regardless of the time.

'Come on, Jacob, wake up. You're late for school!'

Too drowsy to care, I replied with those two words I think everyone can relate to after they wake up in the morning, whether it be for work or school. 'Fuck's sake!'

'Language, young man!'

'Sorry, Mum,' I said groggily. 'I didn't get a good night's sleep.'

'Well, hurry up. Your breakfast is ready and your dad is going to take you to school.'

I immediately thought of Pete. 'Mum,' she stopped halfway at the door with an arm full of washing, 'what happened to Pete and his dad? Are they alright?'

'Hmm… best let your dad explain, but right now you need to get ready,' she said then left, leaving my door half open.

I tried to move hastily, but the lack of energy got the better of me. I didn't eat much breakfast either. I didn't have much of an appetite, not today anyway.

After a quick wash and clumsily put my school clothes on, I headed for the door. Dad was already in the car with the engine running. 'Come on, son. You're late,' he said through the open window.

I replied with a grunt.

On the way to school Dad explained what the outcome was with Pete and his dad's little escapade. He got a late phone call from Mike the night before. I sat there rubbing my brow, trying to nurse a headache. 'You all right, son?' he asked.

My eyes were closed and I didn't look at him when I answered. 'Didn't sleep much,' I said while continuing to rub and knead at my head. 'I'm not feeling very good. Everything happening is taking its toll. Is Pete alright? I can't believe Jonesy's dad would do something like that.'

'Like father, like son,' Dad said. 'Peter's alright. He's a bit black and blue so don't be too shocked when you see him today.'

'He came into school? Why not have the day off?'

Dad shrugged his shoulders, 'You know him, he's eager to learn no matter the cost.'

I screwed up my face as a sharp shooting pain went through my head.

'You sure you're alright, Jacob?'

'Fine, fine.' I kneaded my temples again with my eyes shut.

'I would turn us around and take you home, but your mum would kill me and your exams are coming up, so you need to study as much as you can.'

The word 'study' made my brain throb even more.

'What are your plans after you finish school, son?'

'Do we have to do this now, Dad?'

'Just asking. It's always good to be prepared,' he said, lowering a gear to turn at a junction.

'Well, I hate to disappoint you, but I've got a lot more on my mind right now.'

'Ah, the Jonesy thing.'

'It's a big distraction.'

Dad indicated right and parked in a space just opposite the school doors. The time on the dashboard said 10:06am. I had to move quickly, but Dad started to speak again as I was halfway out the car. 'Jacob, remember what I told you last night. I know you didn't do anything wrong, but don't lose yourself in your own temper and try to keep your cool. We'll sort this all out, try not to worry, son.'

I nodded and replied, 'Thanks, Dad.'

'I'll see you later, son,' and off he went.

Dad was right, I should've been prepared for a living after school, but the years seemed to be flying by which didn't allow me time to prepare for anything.

The main doors of the school seemed quiet and they welcomed me with a menacing smile and a mocking voice that represented a teacher saying, *'You're late, Jacob!'*

I wasn't in the right frame of mind. I had the instinctual nature to look about me and listen for a certain vehicle, but it was nowhere to be seen. Paranoia surged through me – the police could be wanting to question me about the issue in the toilets, but as Dad said, I'd done nothing wrong. I took a deep breath, slouched my bag over my shoulder, and entered.

## 15

The main hall was quiet; all I could hear were the faint voices of teachers instructing their students as I hastily made my way to the office. The door was open and as I entered, I was encountered by a small man with a pot belly sitting at one of the desks shuffling through paperwork. He looked at me as I stood at the door. 'Sorry I'm late,' I said. 'My name's Jacob.'

The man's face changed to disappointment, 'All right. Why are you late?'

'I slept in.'

'Better get to class then, and *don't* do it again,' he said then turned his attention back to his duties.

I walked away without saying another word. He didn't seem to care who I was, the only thing he did care about was his satisfaction of authority.

*Prick.*

I knew walking into class wouldn't be the same as a walk in the park. I got to my designated classroom and looked through the small window of the door. Mrs Hemingway was writing summations on the blackboard, but her hand stopped as I entered. All eyes diverted towards me and Mrs Hemingway glared with disappointment as though waiting for an explanation. 'You're late, Jacob.'

'Sorry, Mrs Hemingway. I didn't sleep well.'

'That's no excuse. Don't let it happen again.'

'Sorry,' I repeated.

'Take a seat,' her eyes indicated my desk. I sat at it and Mrs Hemingway continued.

Regardless of being late, I didn't pay much attention; my mind was elsewhere. I fiddled with my pen, Mrs Hemingway's words muffled to my ears. I looked out the window to my left, my eyes searching for the vehicle. Then they would revert back to the classroom door as though waiting for the police to come barging in and apprehend me for what I'd done to Jonesy in the toilets–

'Jacob, pay attention.'

My mind quickly shifted out of its daze. 'Sorry, Mrs Hemingway.' But I couldn't help it, I was too distracted. I kept thinking of who I could talk to about my predicament. Should I go to the police and tell them I was being stalked? Should I tell my parents? I was desperate to talk to someone, *anyone* about the strange events that had occurred during the past few days. I had to find Pete; he really was the only person I could trust. Although, he was going through a lot right now, no thanks to his dad.

*I wonder how he's doing.*

I still couldn't believe Jonesy's dad punched him.

The school bell rang earlier than usual and I didn't seem to have learnt a thing – hadn't heard one word; in one ear and out the other, so to speak. As the students stood up and gathered their things Mrs Hemingway had something important to say.

'I know it's early, class, but if you please take your lunch break now and when you come back make your way to the canteen for an important announcement. So come back at 12pm and head straight there.'

Was this about what had happened in the toilets? If so, why announce it to everyone? Why exploit it and make matters worse? Jonesy didn't care about discipline. If anything, this would probably fuel his fire against me and Pete.

'What's this for?' one curious student asked Mrs Hemingway.

'Not sure. Miss Clark wants all teachers and students to head there at twelve. To be honest, we're just as curious as you.'

I packed up my things and made for the canteen, but food wasn't really on my mind; I was mostly focused on finding Pete, but he was nowhere to be seen. The only place I could think of was the library; he spent most of his time in that place. I guessed it was his only sanctuary – people like Jonesy wouldn't even dream of stepping foot in a library. He was probably trying to keep a low profile as he probably didn't want too many eyes on his face.

The library wasn't too far from where I was. I hastily walked down the stairs and went out the small door next to the canteen. This brought me outside onto the school yard which was somewhat of a recreational area for students to practice their sports skills. There were small pathways that led into the opposite building. This building was the science wing but had other additional activities such as a small amphitheatre for drama purposes and a decent-sized library.

I took the pathway closest to the door of the library. It opened with a creak, so I had to be careful not to bother the students who were studying. As soon as I closed it, I was enveloped in pure silence and the whiff of books, new and old, that hung in the air. My eyes darted around, scanning the place for my good friend. Just as I suspected, Pete was sitting in one of the small booths with his head down, engrossed in his books, his pen shifting manically as he wrote.

There was an old wrinkly, strict-looking woman standing behind the reception desk. Her glasses, that were held on by a piece of thread, were hanging on the bottom of her nose which caused her head to lower slightly as she eyed me suspiciously. She must've thought I was here to cause trouble as I was very seldom there. I gave her a small smile as I approached Pete, but she just blankly ignored me and continued whatever it was she was doing.

I crept up on him for good humour, 'PETE!'

'Jesus!' he jumped. 'Don't do that.' He looked at the librarian. She shot daggers from those sinister eyes, but Pete gave her an apologetic nod. 'What are you doing here?'

'Looking for you,' I said, seating myself down opposite him while studying his face. 'New glasses?'

'Spare.' He took them off and turned his head slightly to the right to give me a view.

'It doesn't look that bad,' I said.

'My mum put a bit of make up on it to cover a bit of the bruising,' he said while putting his glasses back on.

'You could've had the day off, you know?'

'I know, but our exams are coming up, and I want to do as much studying as I can.'

'What about your dad, is he alright?'

He gave out a disappointed sigh, 'Don't ask. He had to sleep on the couch last night. Mum was furious with him.'

I was silent for a moment then asked, 'Did you hear?'

'About the announcement? Yeah, I heard.'

'Do you think it's about us?'

'Highly unlikely,' Pete said. He was still writing with his head down. 'I don't think they would drag the whole school in one room just to have a talk about it. No, this is something else. Something much bigger and more important than our situation.'

'Like what?'

Pete shrugged his shoulders.

'Have the police spoken to you yet?'

'I've seen enough police to last me a lifetime. If you're referring to Jonesy then no. But his dad on the other hand is a different story.'

'So what happened to him?'

'He's been charged for hitting me, but I think nothing serious will happen.'

'How come?'

'Dad was the one that started it. He went to his house; he was verbally aggressive and the fight commenced. I've never seen him like that before.'

I nodded in agreement. 'Yeah. Paul and the twins have backed off a bit since our encounter in the toilets, but probably still best to keep our distance from them.'

'I think Jonesy is still in hospital or recovering. Maybe the others feel lost now their leader isn't about for the time being.' Pete had sarcasm in his tone. 'But what will happen when he comes back?'

The question was left in the air. I sat back in the chair and let Pete continue with his studies. My fingernails tapped against the table. I tried to speak but couldn't get the words out.

Pete's eyes looked up through his glasses, 'Do you mind? That's really annoying.'

'Uh? Oh, sorry.' I stopped the tapping.

'What's with you today? You look nervous. If you're worried about the police–'

'No, it's not that.'

'Then what is it?' His pen stopped and he looked at me as though waiting for what I had to say.

I moved in closer; my hands reached the centre of the table and I spoke in a low tone, 'I was followed yesterday after school!'

Pete took a moment to process what I'd just said. 'Followed? By who?'

'I don't know.'

He closed his books, straightened his glasses and lent forward on the table, looking intrigued.

'Are you sure you were followed?'

'Believe me, I'm positive I was followed and not just that, they tried to run me down in their car, but I couldn't see their faces.'

'Did you get the reg number?'

'Didn't have time to look.' I paused for a moment, 'Come to think of it, I don't think the vehicle had a reg number.'

Pete stared at me open mouthed. 'What did you do?'

'Well, first they followed me after I got off the bus. I was going to run to my house but led them away.'

'Smart move,' he said.

'That's not the worst of it. They chased me all around town. I came to a dead-end...'

'Then what?'

At least I had got the easy part out the way, but the next part was going be difficult for Pete to comprehend. He waited patiently for me to speak again. 'I noticed a large wooden fence, about ten-feet in height. As soon as I knew it, I was in mid-air, jumping over it.'

'Jumped? You mean climbed?'

He saw in my eyes that I meant what I said. He sat back in his chair, took his glasses off and rubbed the bridge of his nose. He winced, forgetting about his bruise. Confused as he was, I knew what he was thinking: is it possible for a boy of my stature to jump clean over a ten-foot fence? I knew it wasn't impossible to climb over it. Take parkour for instance: the individual would run, jump and quickly place one foot on the fence to give him that extra leverage, place his hands at the top and jump over. All these things were understandable and explainable, but how did you explain someone in my situation jumping a ten-foot fence in one fluid motion, without placing a hand or foot on it?

Pete was now cautiously rubbing his eyes. He put his glasses back on and spoke. 'To anyone else, it doesn't seem believable, but in your case, there's an exception.' I was surprised to hear this from his lips. He saw my confusion so he explained. 'You remember when Jonesy chased you that day on our bikes?

I nodded.

'Your speed didn't seem normal. And the toilets? Your strength was…'

'I know. What I felt back then was the same feeling only it lasted longer. I was running the same speed as the vehicles, and it was a 30 zone.'

All this came down to a question that he'd already asked me before – the only question that would explain my strange attributes. 'Are you sure you're not on drugs?'

'PETE, I'M NOT–' he interrupted me by putting his finger to his lips to silence me. I looked at the librarian; she shot daggers once again. I'd almost forgotten where I was for a moment. I looked back at Pete and spoke in a quieter manner, 'I'm not on drugs!'

'Okay, sorry. I believe you, but what do you expect? We do have to look at the possibilities of what's causing this to happen.'

'I know, but something is happening to me. I don't know what, but I feel different these days.'

'Different? how?'

'Well, I can hear things from afar.'

'How far?'

'Quite far. How else do you think I found you when you were being attacked in the toilets? I was in the canteen when that happened.'

The school toilets weren't that far from the canteen, but with multiple voices running through the air it would make it quite difficult for anyone to hear a thing in the adjacent rooms.

Pete was about to speak again but was interrupted by the school bell. Our conversation was over, but I knew my situation was a lot to take in for him, and in a way, he was right. You had to look at all possibilities and explanations. I glanced at the library clock. It was 12pm.

*The announcement!*

We both collected our bags and made our way to the canteen.

## 16

The canteen had doors on each side of the massive room and these doors were flooded with students hanging around to be seated or find a reasonable space to stand as they waited on the school's rector to speak.

Pete and I were waiting at the doors as the queue slowly moved. I caught a glimpse of a police officer through a small gap. He was standing with his arms crossed, looking around the canteen. I became nervous as a few more officers came into sight. I turned and spoke to Pete. He looked as nervous as I was. 'What do you think this is all about?'

'I'm not sure.'

'Remember, we did nothing wrong,' I said. But I found it odd that Pete was nervous considering what he had said earlier in the library; this did seem much bigger and important. I guessed part of him didn't believe that.

The smell of food not long cooked lingered in the air. There was a mixture of deep-fried foods: chips, roast potatoes and others;

steamed veg from whatever kind of soup and there was the final touch of coffee which emanated its bitter scent from the machines.

We stood almost at the back, making sure we were incognito, avoiding being the centre of attention. The air was warm considering the mass of bodies that occupied the place. School-bags were thrown to the floor and left in a haphazard state as the owners found their seats or stood in any space they could find. It was like being at a concert.

Hundreds of voices pervaded the air as students held their own conversations. The volume reverberated around the room, gradually breaking down into silence after being interrupted by another, powerful voice, 'QUIET! QUIET!'

We all looked in the direction of the speaker; it was Mr Smith, the rector of the school. He was a tall intimidating man dressed in a white shirt with a black tie. His natural hair colour was disguised with a bleach-blond, judging by his dark eyebrows and chest hair sprouting out the top of his shirt. He was Miss Clark's boss, and I think she was intimidated by him, and she didn't take shit from anyone.

Only rarely would we see this man. However, if it was something important then that was when he would appear. He was the kind of person with nothing but domination and authority on his mind.

Mr Smith was accompanied by Miss Clark at his side. A few other teachers were also present. And to make matters worse, the two police officers were standing next to one another holding their hats. They all stood next to the food-serving area.

Mr Smith was the one to speak first. 'I believe most of you are well aware of the situation regarding the people that've gone missing during the last month. For those of you that are completely oblivious to this—' Mr Smith's eyes locked on to a few students that were chatting away to themselves—'then I suggest you pay attention to what these officers have to say.'

The students stopped bickering and remained silent.

One of the officers that I'd recognised a long time ago, stepped forward and introduced himself as Inspector Gregory. 'Thank you, Mr Smith. I know some of you may be scared or confused, but believe me, we're taking drastic protocols for you and your families' safety. We're going to apply specific rules that I would appreciate you follow. There's a curfew that's going to take place.' Many students obviously weren't happy about this and the officer earned himself a reply of sighs.

'QUIET!' Mr Smith commanded.

The Inspector continued. 'The curfew is going to take place as soon as school finishes so I'd suggest getting on the bus and going straight home. For those of you walking home, try to stay in a well-lit area – preferably a main street. Do *not* go down any dark alleys or places where there is no light, I can't emphasise that enough. Our vehicles will be patrolling certain parts of the city and there'll be officers on foot. So please, for your safety, go straight home and stay indoors. If there's anyone that is not indoors during the curfew time then they'll be picked up immediately and taken back to their homes. We'll notify you when the curfew is lifted.'

Mr Smith stepped in again. 'Thank you, Inspector Gregory. I hope you all have been paying attention. Remember, the same rule applies to all of us, so don't feel like you're the only ones. And if you have any questions, please speak to Inspector Gregory and his partner, Constable Michaelson. If not, go back to class.'

Some teachers left and students stood up to gather their belongings, muttering and moaning. But Pete and I felt relieved considering the announcement wasn't about us. But this was bigger than we'd thought. I'd seen it on the news and now it was affecting all of us with a curfew set in place.

Pete and I made our way back to our specific classes, but our minds were not at ease. 'So, what's happening with our problem?' Pete asked.

'I'm not sure. We should try and speak with Miss Clark.' Just as I said this, Miss Clark was making her way through a crowd of students.

'Excuse me, excuse me,' she demanded.

'Miss Clark! Miss Clark!' I shouted.

She turned and faced me. 'Oh, Jacob. Look, I'm kind of busy, so if you have any questions ask the police officers—'

'No, no, it's not about that. It's about the other day – about what happened in the toilets.'

'Ah yes. Well, we've notified your parents about it.'

'But what about the police?'

'We've mentioned it, but they can't do anything. They think of it as students in disagreement with one another, that's all.'

'But Jonesy pulled a knife on us, not to mention his dad hit Pete,' I said frustratingly.

Miss Clark gazed over my shoulder towards Pete. 'I'm so sorry for what happened to you, Peter. Unfortunately, the situation has escalated and is in the police's hands now. And due to this new situation that's just come up, they kind of have their hands full.

'So for the time being, they have bigger problems to deal with. I assure you, Jacob, we'll look into your issue ASAP. Now, if you'll excuse me, I'm very busy.' Miss Clark turned and disappeared in amongst a crowd of bodies that stood near the exits of the canteen.

'What'd she say?' Pete asked from behind me.

I just stared on. *We'll look into it.* I'd heard this saying so many times, but nothing was ever done about it.

'Jacob?' Pete's voice broke my thoughts.

'She said she'll look into it.'

## 17

The rest of the day passed swiftly. Everywhere we went, students were gossiping about the news, some with faces of fear and worry; others – the mindless and ignorant – thought it quite amusing. None of us seemed too eager to learn anything that day and the teachers tried in vain to make us pay attention. I just kept my head down as usual, scribbling notes on my jotter, but I abruptly came to a stop as my head was suddenly filled with a sharp, acute pain. I kneaded my temples as my eyes clamped shut.

'Jacob, you all right?' Mrs Monroe said.

'No, not really. My head…' I tried to show my manners and look at her while I spoke, but my vision was compromised by the excruciating pain forcing me to close them again.

'Your head? Do you have a headache?'

'You could say that.'

'Oh! You better go take a timeout with some fresh air. If you're not any better, see the school nurse, she should give you something for it. But remember, you've only got thirty minutes until school finishes. You can't be late for your bus.'

'Yeah, thanks, Mrs Monroe.' I hastily moved towards the door with my hands shielding my eyes. I felt the students' eyes on my back and heard a few sniggers here and there that were obviously aimed at my uncoordinated behaviour, but I didn't care; all I cared about was getting rid of this blinding pain.

I managed to find the toilets with slight difficulty considering my limited vision. I clumsily pushed the door open and stumbled towards the sink. Projectile vomit spewed from my mouth and splashed into the sink. I took a moment to breathe as my whole body was drenched in sweat. I ran the cold water tap to wash away the vomit – the smell and sight made me want to heave again. I cupped my hands together, placed them under the tap to collect the water and poured it over my face.

The feeling was invigorating; the pressure in my head started to subside and the overwhelming feeling of sickness was fading. I stood there for a few minutes, looking in the mirror as I took in deep breaths that helped settle my stomach. I splashed my face again, however, as soon as I stood up straight and my eyes opened to my reflection, I realised I wasn't alone.

I turned to face a man and recognition dawned. He was tall with short black hair and his face was bristly and worn-looking. But he still looked the same as when he and Dad had confronted each other. Age had given him a few wrinkles here and there, but he still looked to be an intelligent man. His expression was sombre, like he was studying me. He appeared to be in a state of wonderment.

'You!' I exclaimed.

He took a step closer towards me, his eyes regarding my own. 'Please, don't be afraid. I'm here to help you, Jacob,' he said.

'Help me? Who the fuck are you? And how do you know my name?' I said, cautiously and slowly making my way to the door.

'My name is Gary Macleod. Please, Jacob, don't run. I'm not going to hurt you. You must listen to me, there's not much time.' His movements were becoming jittery and a nervous tick fluttered in the corner of one eye.

'Not much time for what?'

'Not here; it's not safe.'

He had to be suffering from some kind of delusional state or some other mental issue. My efforts communicating with him were at an end and I made my way to the door, but his next words stopped me from opening it.

'Tell me, Jacob, are you experiencing headaches?'

My hand let go of the door-handle and I turned to face him as he continued. 'Do you hear things more clearly that no one else can? Can you smell things from afar when you put your mind to it?'

'How do you know that?'

Gary smiled, 'I know a lot about you, Jacob. And I know what's happening to you.'

This time, I took a step towards him, 'Who are you?'

'Like I said: my name is Gary Macleod. I'm a scientist. I've been watching you for a very long time.'

'Why?'

'To make sure you're safe.'

'Safe from what?'

Gary let out a disappointed sigh. 'My brother, Terry – your biological dad,' his voice was low and flat.

I stared at him in awe for a moment. 'I don't understand. What do you want me to say? You're talking about someone I've never even met and in case you've forgotten, I was adopted. I'm sure you remember that from when you came to my house years ago and frightened my family.'

Gary became frustrated, 'I was trying to warn them, but they wouldn't listen. You have no idea what my brother is capable of. You think everything happening to you has no meaning? It does! Your muscular form. Your senses. And the two men that have been stalking you—'

I stopped him there, 'What did you say?'

'Oh yes. I know about those two men who have been hassling you.'

'Who are they?'

'Let's just say they're associates of Terry's. After hearing about your little encounter with them, I had to make contact with you.'

So there had been two of them in that vehicle. 'What do they want and why were they trying to kill me?'

'They weren't trying to kill you. They were testing you.'

'For what?'

'Your endurance. Your capabilities.'

I was completely puzzled and Gary saw it. He continued, 'They tested your capabilities: your speed, strength and power. And now it's apparent they know what you're capable of. But this is only the beginning.'

'The beginning of what?'

'Not here, Jacob. Quickly, come with me.'

He took hold of my arm, but I shoved it off. 'Let go of me, I'm not going anywhere with you.'

'Look, I can explain everything but not here. Please, you must come with me, now!' Gary was persistent and wouldn't let go of my arm. I shoved him once more and made for the toilet door. He followed and stopped at the door and shouted, 'You're going to become something powerful, Jacob. And you can't stop it!'

His voice echoed throughout the hallway as I ran away. A petite blonde-haired teacher came out from a nearby classroom to see what all the commotion was. 'What's going on here?' she said as I took refuge by her side. She noticed my distress and looked in the direction I came from. Her eyes fell on Gary. 'Excuse me, but who are you? And why are you bothering a pupil?'

Gary didn't say anything; he just took one last glance at me and ran the other way.

'Are you all right?' the teacher asked.

'I'm fine.' It was hard to believe what Gary had said, but a lot of it rang true. But ultimately, I wasn't going to follow some man I'd just met even if he was trying to help me. How could I trust him?

By the end of the day, the school was in upheaval. The police were suspicious after the situation with Gary, speculating there was a connection between him and the missing individuals, but I thought otherwise. Gary didn't seem the kidnapping type. It was maybe just pure coincidence he'd shown up at the wrong place at the wrong time.

The police were now on high alert and watched the building like hawks, carefully patrolling the school grounds. It kind of felt like a prison. Teachers were also looking over their shoulders after exiting the school as they hastily made their ways to their cars. It was no longer just on the news; now it was on their doorstep.

The curfew was in effect; school was over for the day, and teachers and students made their way home post-haste. I thought of the latter, going through their front doors, slamming them shut and locking them, with their parents keeping a close eye on them. My little town would be a ghost town.

The students had all left the school and I was the only one that remained, staying behind to give a statement. Even after the news about the curfew, the police understood that I could be an asset to them. Furthermore, they were going to drive me home after my questioning just to provide my safety. I also took the opportunity to consult the school nurse regarding my head. The pain was becoming unbearable and I had to get something to ease it.

My statement took place in Miss Clark's office. The teacher that had come to my aid during my encounter with Gary sat next to me on the couch as she was a witness to the affair. Gregory and his partner Sergeant Michaelson arrived immediately after being informed of the news. I felt like an infant again.

The Inspector stood there with pen and notepad at the ready. Miss Clark sat at her desk and Mr Smith stood next to the two officers looking dominant as usual, hands in pockets as he surveyed the situation intently.

'I tried calling your parents to let them know about the situation, but there was no answer,' Miss Clark said.

I just nodded. I was too busy rubbing my eyes, trying to nurse the headache. It throbbed and caused my concentration to be a little lax, but the police were desperate for me to give them any valuable information that could be useful to them.

'So, from the beginning,' Gregory said, 'what did this man look like?'

'He was, he looked like...' I struggled to find my words. Thinking hurt like hell and I started to rub my temples.

The teacher that sat next to me stepped in. '…He was tall with black hair.' All eyes turned towards her as she continued, 'He wore a brown jacket with a white T-shirt underneath, and his jeans were navy blue.'

Gregory stepped closer. He passed his pen and notepad to Michaelson, and, like when I was younger, asked in his usual sympathetic manner, 'Are you feeling all right, son?' He knew this wasn't the first time I had encountered this man; he still had to ask what he'd looked like as the years may have taken their toll on Gary.

He must've thought I was suffering from a state of shock. 'I'm fine,' I said, 'just a headache, that's all.'

Coincidently, there was a knock on the office door and the nurse's head poked in. She was a stout woman who didn't seem to possess any sign of a bedside manner. Her facial expression was stern as she walked in the room. 'Sorry to interrupt. I have some painkillers for Jacob.'

She had them in one hand and a glass of water in the other and hastily brought them over to me. 'I'd advise you to see your doctor ASAP. I think you might be suffering from migraines,' she said unsympathetically.

I gave her an acknowledged nod and she exited the room but not without a quick reply from Miss Clark saying, 'Thank you.'

The nurse left the room without acknowledge her.

As I took the painkillers, the Inspector continued with more questions. 'So what exactly did this Gary Macleod say to you?'

'He said he was a scientist.'

'A scientist? What kind of scientist?'

'He didn't say.'

'I see. What else did he say?'

'He said that…' I hesitated for a moment. No one knew I was adopted, but I had no choice about mentioning it, '…he said he was the brother of my real dad.'

'I don't understand. So he's your uncle?'

'Yes. I mean no. I don't know!' I leaned forward and placed my head on my hands.

Gregory spoke in his kind tone again. 'I know you're feeling frustrated, Jacob, but we need to know the smallest details and any information that could be useful to catch this guy.'

I raised my head and my eyes caught his. 'I'm adopted.'

'I'm sorry?' Gregory craned his head so he could hear my repeated words.

'I'm adopted.' The people in the room heard and exchanged surprised glances.

Both officers were taken aback and took a moment to comprehend my predicament. I continued. 'This isn't my first encounter with Gary. He came to my house when I was a kid claiming he was the brother of my real dad. And now he's back!'

Gregory wasn't surprised, but Mr Smith intervened, 'But why now, after all these years?'

I wanted to answer; I wanted to mention about my heightened senses, but then the conversation would become too complex and I was more focused on getting home.

'Maybe his biological parents found him and tried an unorthodox method of getting him back.' It was Miss Clark that answered Mr Smith's question.

'You can't be serious?' Mr Smith said.

'It's known to happen.'

Gregory spoke, 'Did he say the name of your real dad?'

'I...I don't remember, it all happened too fast,' I said, rubbing my brow.

He watched me nurse my head; he knew I couldn't withstand more questions, 'I think it's best to call it a night for now. We'll look into this Gary Macleod and we can deal with it tomorrow with clear heads. It's been a long and stressful day for all of us. We'll take you home, Jacob, just to be on the safe side.'

'Thank you,' I said faintly.

As we made our way outside, the hallway lights were blinding, like knives slowly twisting their way into my eyes and into my skull. I felt as though I was under arrest with the two officers at each side of me. I was grateful the school was quiet otherwise students would've had an interesting topic to discuss.

Michaelson placed her hand on my head and said, 'Mind your head,' as she escorted me inside the vehicle. I guess it had become a natural thing for them considering that most of the people they put inside their vehicles were criminals. In my situation, it felt as though I was in a witness protection programme.

The journey home had a relaxing effect on me as the vehicle drove smoothly towards my house.

Gregory asked the odd question about his case but became silent after noticing I had become unresponsive. My head was slumped against the window and I stared out at the vista which was mesmerising. My eye-lids started to become heavy and eventually shut.

## 19

From the moment my eyes closed, I slipped into the same familiar dream. Only this time, there was no running; there was no sign of fear; there was only me standing solo in an inky-darkness. I viewed my hands… they were human. I barely had the time to observe my surroundings when, without warning, I felt teeth clamping themselves to my throat. It was the same creature that had been haunting me from my previous dreams. I managed a quick look at my unknown enemy and made out some more of its features: K-9 teeth, a snout, large ears, fur.

The dream took on a drastic change. Not only did the creature's teeth sink into me, but its head, arms and legs somehow fused themselves with my own, causing both our bodies to become one grotesque amorphous mass. Subconsciously, my mind was in pain as our bodies became one and as this performance reached its zenith, I felt nothing but pure euphoria. I was me again, but my mind and body appeared to be something else. Something… something…

'… Jacob, Jacob?' A distinct voice came. My body flinched as I escaped the dream world. 'Bad dream?' The Inspector was looking at me from the passenger seat with a small smile on the side of his face. 'We're here,' he said.

'Thanks.' I opened the door, but Gregory spoke again.

'Remember, try and not think about what happened today. I know it's scary, but we'll deal with it ASAP. You have yourself a good rest and we'll be in contact if need be, okay, Jacob?'

'Yeah, thank you,' I said wearily.

I closed the door behind me and the police car drove off. I was hoping Mum hadn't seen me getting dropped off by the authorities. She would be furious and just get herself in a frantic state.


I felt nauseous as I walked the short distance to my house; my legs felt like jelly, my bones ached and my head still throbbed. The after-effects of that strange turn I'd had in the school toilets were somehow staying with me, and it seemed like it wasn't going to subside anytime soon. The nurse's advice came to mind: I should really see a doctor ASAP.

I rubbed the right side of my head to try and ease the pain – thinking too much hurt. Shit! I didn't even know what time it was. As I drunkenly weaved from side-to-side, something disturbed my train of thought. I stopped in my tracks as my eyes gazed at the familiar dark vehicle. It was parked a few feet away from my house. I approached it with caution to get a closer look just to be sure it was the same one I'd previously encountered. I was curious to see inside it, but fear was holding me back.

Each step felt like a struggle, but I stopped walking after I heard my house door being opened. I was expecting Mum and Dad to come out to confront me about my whereabouts but no. It wasn't them; it was two suspicious-looking men leaving my house in a discreet fashion. I darted behind a couple of bins and crouched down. Fortunately, they didn't see me. I peeked out and watched…

From what I could gather, they were both bald and wore black suits. I pressed my back against the bins as much as I could in case they spotted me. My breathing became uncontrollable and loud, but the sound was covered just in time by their car coming to life. It revved a few times and they drove off.

I stepped out from the bins, the remnants of the vehicle's exhaust fumes lingering in the air. How did they know where I lived? I was almost certain I had led them away from the house during my last encounter.

My eyes turned to focus on my house; the door was slightly ajar as if it was giving me a welcoming gesture – an ominous one. My head span as fatigue and nausea took their toll.

The door was heavy as I pushed it open; it gave off a long, slow creak. I stared into the lobby. All seemed completely normal. I closed the door behind me and quickly locked it. I expected Mum to come stampeding towards me, shouting, 'Where have you been?', but she didn't appear.

My clothes were clinging to my skin and my body felt clammy. My heart rate was still racing and I could hear the beats in the quietness. I stood there inside my house, listening and waiting. Silence.

I made my way to the kitchen. Dishes were stacked up in the basin and there was food on a plate which was wrapped in cling film. Even though Mum cooked healthy, tasty meals, the thought of eating there and then turned my stomach. Had I contracted some sort of fever? I felt bad knowing she had cooked my tea and I wasn't even there; I was late again.

I left the kitchen and returned to the lobby. 'Mum? Dad? You here?' No reply. I then heard a faint sound coming from the living room: it was the TV. I pushed the living room door open, but the lights were off. I turned them on. 'Mum? Da–?'

No one should have to witness the horror that faced me as I approached the bodies of my parents. My eyes saw them, but my brain couldn't comprehend it. *This is a dream, this can't be real!*

My body became limp, deprived of its equilibrium and my legs were no longer able to hold me upright. I fell next to the lifeless bodies. My hand touched a warm liquid. I stared at my bloody hand in disbelief as blood kept soaking the light-grey carpet. I wanted to avert my eyes from the bodies but I was transfixed. I wanted to hold them, comfort them and also wake up from this horrid nightmare. But there was no waking up from this. Part of me still believed there would be a sign of life; any sign at all.

Mum lay there on her stomach next to the couch in a large pool of blood with what appeared to be two exit wounds protruding from her back and head. Dad seemed to have shared the same fate.

He was sitting on his recliner with a bullet wound to the chest and head. The image of his mangled face was horrific, unbearable. Part of me was grateful Mum's was face down.

I clumsily leaned back against the couch and placed my hand to my mouth to try and control the vomit swirling around in my stomach. I tried looking elsewhere, but the images refused to go away. Tears fell down my cheeks, building to a wail. Slowly, sadness was replaced by anger, anger was then replaced with rage.

The phone rang. I struggled to pick it up from the side of the couch but eventually placed it to my ear. 'Hello? Hello? Is Jacob there?' It was Pete. Probably calling to discuss the announcement, and the situation with Jonesy, but my mind wasn't in the right place.

I couldn't find my words. 'Pete,' I said in distress.

'Jacob. You all right?'

'Pete. Something… something's happened.'

'What? Jacob? JACOB?'

I lost my train of thought. My mind went blank and the phone fell from my hand. And then, abruptly, my body was struck with a surge of pain, causing me to bend over double. I screamed as tears ran down my face. I thrashed from side-to-side as the pain intensified. The symptoms I'd previously experienced were once again in effect, but oddly profound and out of control. I tried to remember my breathing techniques, but they were overpowered by the images of Mum and Dad.

Something was burning inside me. My body was now on all fours and it started to tremble. My mind raced with thoughts – ruminating all the negative things that had antagonized me: Jonesy, Gary, Pete getting attacked in the school toilets and, of course, the two strange men that had just murdered my parents. I could still hear Pete's voice constantly repeating my name through the receiver, but I was incapable of responding.

These thoughts that raced through my head somehow fused themselves together, causing my body to hit a point of no return. The trembling became worse, sweat was pouring off me and then a sharp shooting pain originated around the spinal area.

*My God! What's happening to me?*

My body was changing, starting to alter itself. I screamed out with excruciating pain as I felt and heard "snaps" that exploded in the air. My spinal column shattered multiple times as each segment reshaped themselves one-by-one. My insides felt like they were on fire as my bones slowly broke, twisted themselves and became elongated.

I struggled to see what was happening to me – to see if there was any way I could prevent it. I watched as my hands changed themselves into something that seemed unbelievable and incomprehensible. Finger tips were gradually replaced with claws and a light-brown fur coated my hands.

*Help me! Help ME!*

My arms snapped in an irregular form: they slowly thickened and rearranged themselves. As my whole anatomy took on this change, my clothes ripped from my body as it became increasingly larger in size.

Meanwhile, my skull felt as though the bones were tearing through the epidermis. My jawbone grew tremendously in size, and huge sharp teeth poked at my tongue. It was a slow, agonizing process as my cranium continued its malformation. I screamed once more and, as I did, my vocal cords became distorted and it wasn't the scream of a man but that of something else – something beastly!

The pain had diminished and it was as though something lying dormant had been awoken. My body felt as though it had transcended itself into a higher plane of existence – a euphoric state! I quickly stood up, banging my head against the ceiling. Dazed and confused at this clumsiness, I realised I was taller. My hands – they had claws where the nails should be and were coated in the same kind of fur as my arms. I lost my balance again due to frightful panic and as I did, my eyes landed on the oval-shaped mirror hanging on the wall just above the mantelpiece. Staring back at me was a creature that resembled a wolf.

It appeared uncanny yet benevolent as I studied my new-found features. *My God, what has happened to me? What have I become?*

My body was overlaid in the same kind of fur as that of my arms and it also appeared to have taken on a muscular tone from what I could make out in the mirror. I kept telling myself it was some kind of hallucination or a dream, but I remembered that my dreams didn't exactly show any kind of refuge.

A sudden realisation came to my mind: was this the beast from my dreams? Considering how strange this was, the similarities of the transformation were, to my knowledge, common to that of a lycanthrope. The creature I'd become didn't seem to be nightmarish in the least. I knew this was debatable because werewolves were typically ruthless, sinister creatures that focused only on killing their prey. They were known to be remorseless killing predators. But in my case, I still possessed my human characteristics and faculties. My attributes appeared anthropomorphic, therefore I was still in control. That left one question: what was I?

After studying myself and with my mind racing with questions, I remembered Mum and Dad. My gaze landed on the bodies that lay before me. Both still. Their bodies, now a crimson pool, fuelled me with rage. My face tightened, my fists clenched and an intimidating growl came from my throat. Instinct kicked in!

I didn't want to leave them, but it was either stay and do nothing or retribution. After all, *I* now owned the advantage. *I* was going to be the predator that stalked its prey at night. And my prey was two strange men.

I regained my composure and with a quick, fluid-like motion, I ran to my front door and did not stop. My body charged through it like a juggernaut and it smashed to pieces as if it was paper. My mind was hell-bent on catching the two murderers and nothing was going to stop me. Nothing!

## 20

I moved with haste as I hunted the two men on the streets. I started in the quiet neighbourhood near my house moving from shadow-to-shadow and worked my way to the high street. I sniffed and listened for any indication of the two culprits' whereabouts. My senses were stronger than ever and my hearing seemed to have quadrupled. It picked up the sounds of multiple car engines driving back and forth through the town and random voices that held different conversations. My sense of smell was 100 times keener and I picked up a dozen of them: exhaust fumes from vehicles; smoke that spewed from chimneys; food from the local chip shop and other smells that I couldn't distinguish lingered in the air as I moved.

Furthermore, after leaving my house and entering the dark shadows, my eyesight had taken on an interesting change. This, I could only assume, was a formation of tapetum lucidum (a tissue that formed behind the retina) which enabled my vision to become improved, especially at night. Some animals possess this tissue but humans on the other hand do not. The vision I was now experiencing was like daylight, cutting through the darkness. Ultimately, my senses had increased significantly and it seemed like a good time to put them to the test.

My neighbourhood was quiet, but the number of people grew as I neared the high street. As I continued to move swiftly in the shadows, I became distracted by startled screams. I'd been spotted by the public. People saw me and immediately ran. After all, it was hard to stay incognito considering my size. I paid no heed to the people's cries and just ran in the direction of the high street.

Some were startled and ran off, shouting for help, while others were puzzled and shared comments about my appearance. But I still paid no attention to them; these people were not my enemy.

It became complicated when I finally reached the main road of the town. Vehicles were coming from both directions with their headlights blinding me. They swerved and lost control, clashing with one another and spraying particles along the road and pavement. Cars further behind ground to a halt. The drivers exited their vehicles to view me in an awed manner.

The whole scene was becoming a catastrophic disaster area. The small town didn't deserve this and it was partially my fault. I could see that some people were injured, not too severely, though. The vehicles closest to me had suffered the worst. One man in particular was still alive but unconscious; I could hear his heartbeat. The other driver was trapped. There was a streak of blood running down the side of his face and he started to panic. 'Help me. Someone help!' he pleaded.

No one helped as the people on the street were mesmerized by the creature that stood before them. I had to intervene. The driver-side door was mangled. I could see the occupant of the vehicle try to shove it open, but it wouldn't budge. His shoving ceased as I approached the door. The driver froze instantaneously, his eyes widening as he witnessed my tall altered stature. I gripped hold of the door and effortlessly ripped it off its hinges and it went flying a few yards behind me. I sensed a bit of relief in the driver as he was free from what might have been his doom.

As I continued my search, people started to help the injured and the man that was trapped. They were probably questioning my motive – my intentions. There was no more I could do at the scene, so I decided to focus on my goal and let the paramedics take over as soon as they arrived which I assumed would be soon.

The air was thick with different smells, making it hard to pinpoint the two men. I tried to focus my hearing, but the sounds of the town were distracting. People were shouting and screaming from the aftermath of the accident; cars were honking their horns and sirens were now audible, building to a crescendo in my head.

The sights and sounds were almost becoming unbearable. I was getting nowhere as I concentrated my senses, but, eventually, I heard two distinct voices over the others. They appeared to be having a conversation – though it wasn't your typical conversation. There was malice in these voices, a sense of menace.

I strained my ears to listen and heard them speak, 'Do you think it will work, sir?'

I heard some sort of static interference – a radio? *'Are you questioning me?'*

'No, sir, I just think—' the man was interrupted by the voice on the radio.

*'Well, don't think; you're not paid to think. You're only to eliminate the targets and get out and you have succeeded, so your job is done.'*

'Yes, sir. Of course. Just one more question, sir?'

'*Proceed.*'

'What's the protocol if the subject pursues?'

'*He's not to be harmed in any way whatsoever. And don't refer to him as the subject!*'

'Yes, sir.'

The conversation with the mysterious voice ended and another began. 'Not to be harmed? What happens if he does pursue?' the voice said apprehensively.

'It won't come to that,' the other said.

'Didn't you see the way he moved before? No one can move like that, not to mention the way he jumped that fence. If the elimination of his parents caused some sort of change then imagine what he could be like, what he'll be able to do?'

'You need to relax,' the voice said calmly. 'We did our part, now it's up to our employer.'

The two voices were silent, but, somehow, I was able to pinpoint their location and made my move towards them.

The bottom of the street became a mass of objects that were now spread in an intricate pattern: cars and people, some still approaching, others trying to get away and the authorities approaching en masse.

My way was restricted; I had to find an easier, clearer path.

From my hiding place, I spotted some fire stairs attached to a block of flats. They were across the road from where I stood. This would give me access to the rooftops and a chance to roam without being seen. But I would have to expose myself in the open street once again to reach them. I had to be quick as people were talking to the police and pointing their fingers in my direction, forcing the officers' eyes to follow. I didn't want to cause more trouble and I certainly didn't want people to fear me.

My time was up: a few officers were coming my way. My body was poised then abruptly jumped out from the shadows. The police stopped in their tracks as I swiftly jumped from car-to-car without a thought. Clearing the last car, I made an attempt to make the final leap towards the fire stairs. My arms caught hold of the metal bars. I didn't use the stairs as any normal human would do; instead, I jumped from level-to-level. My hands gripped the bars; I placed my feet on the others and pushed and repeated with perfect ease until I was at the top.

My path was clear as I reached the rooftop. The sounds from below reverberated throughout the street, but I was able to move freely without being hassled. My strides became a jog and as I concentrated on listening, my ears pricked themselves up to locate the sound of the two men. I soon picked up their voices which enabled my body to follow, like some kind of tracker. My jog turned into a run until it became strenuous then the adrenaline kicked in. I was faced with another state of euphoria as I sprinted along the rooftops. This, I could only guess, was the endorphins released from my brain causing an analgesic effect, establishing the runners' high.

After running and jumping over rooftops, my eyes became focused on a specific car in the distance. It was nearing the end of the town and the rooftops were coming to an end. I had to do something quick or else I was going to lose them.

As I continued my sprint, instinctively, my posture moved its position. My back arched itself as the top half of my body bent forward. My hands outstretched until they made contact with the ground. From plantigrade to digitigrade; from bipedalism to quadrupedalism; I was running on all fours.

My speed increased significantly and my agility and tech-niques were that of a free-runner. I moved swiftly, dodging and jumping objects. I jumped from roof-to-roof and landed with per-fect ease and continued the sprint.

The car was within range in no time, but the rooftops weren't going to last long. In the distance, all I could see was open space: trees, fields and small quiet roads that led into the coun-tryside.

I glanced to my left and the BMW was now parallel with me. I had no plan. Every action I executed was all based on instinct, but there were options: stop, climb down the buildings and do things the slow way and risk losing them, or jump...

The end of the rooftops was near; I was running out of ground. My eyes locked onto the car then back at the edge of the building to pinpoint the exact time to make the leap.

I had to increase my speed so that I was slightly ahead of them. I had to time this right.

*It was now or never!*

My arms stretched towards the sky as my legs pushed like a spring. My body leaped over the edge and I was momentarily in mid-air. As the free-fall commenced, I started to feel the profound, sinking sensation of "butterflies in the stomach".

I viewed the ground from beneath my feet; it was quickly getting closer, but just before I landed on it, SMASH! My leap was perfect timing. My feet came in contact with the roof and it buckled under me, causing the side windows to shatter from the pressure. The car momentarily swerved and bounced from left to right, almost flipping over.

The driver sped up, their quivering voices shouting out expletives.

'It's him!' one of them said.

'Then shake him off.'

The driver quickly veered to the left and right once again in a continuous fashion. I held on for dear life as my body jolted from side-to-side. The wind became intense, its powerful force tumultuous due to the speed that we were going. The vehicle straightened then made its way towards a couple of bins which hit the front of the car. They sprung upwards and clipped me. The car burst through a weak-looking wooden fence, destroying it and spraying me with small splinters.

On the other side of the road was a large brick wall. The car made contact and its side scraped it, sending sparks flying as metal and mortar made contact.

I wasn't getting anywhere; if I was going to make my move I had to wait for the right moment.

The vehicle was heading across to the other side of the road; time to take my chances. With great force, my fist burst through the roof. I heard the passenger shout out as the driver was still trying to shake me off, but his efforts were in vain. There was no way I was letting go. My hand felt around blindly inside hoping it would grab one of them. Eventually, it gripped what felt like an arm, giving me an opportunity to dig my claws into cloth and skin. I retracted my hand and heard the sound of fabric and flesh being torn. My claws and fingers were now crimson.

*Bleed, you bastards.*

There was a loud deafening noise, followed swiftly by another. Two small bullet holes appeared on the roof. 'Stop! He doesn't want him harmed, remember?'

Oncoming traffic peeped their horns as we avoided contact.

'Then what the fuck do we do?'

'Brake, BRAKE!'

The car skidded and abruptly came to a stop. My body tumbled over the windshield and landed on the ground. I stood up unscathed and my eyes locked on my foes. Their headlights showed off my body in all its glory and they stared at me wide-eyed. They probably hadn't expected this when they'd murdered my parents; I guess I'd caught them off guard.

The man on the passenger side broke out of his trance and shouted to the driver, 'Go,' but the driver was still mesmerized.

'GO,' the passenger repeated. The driver became lucid and his foot slammed down hard on the accelerator.

My legs bent then jumped until my body was on the bonnet of the moving vehicle. With a clenched fist, I started to punch the already weakened windshield. I thrived as their faces and screams were in frightful panic as their bodies pushed back into the seats to avoid being harmed. My fist eventually made it through the windshield and I took hold of the driver's shirt and quickly pulled before he had time to brake again. His body shattered the windshield completely before his body fell in front of the still moving vehicle. Just before it lost control, there was a large bump and the sound of bones being crushed.

The man in the passenger seat took hold of the steering wheel to maintain the vehicle's stability; he screamed as the car lost control and I quickly jumped off. It swerved to the right, crashed through another wooden fence until it was greeted by a thick tree.

I watched with satisfaction as I stood on the outskirts of Newburgh. The road was quiet, but it was surely only a matter of time before another vehicle approached. I turned, about to walk away, when I heard a faint murmur coming from the car.

The faint cries for help seemed to possess no strength at all.

I approached the car, the cries becoming louder. The thing was totalled. The smell of its sizzling steaming engine was strong – what was left of it. The whole front part was embedded almost within the tree.

I stood at the passenger side and ripped the door off. The man in the passenger seat was near death, his head against the de-flated air-bag in a bloody mess. 'Please, help me,' he gurgled as blood spewed from his mouth. His eyes regarded me and he fell into frightful hysteria, realising his life was about to end. I took hold of his throat; he kicked and screamed as I yanked him out of his seat.

His screams were now restricted as my hands were wrapped around his throat. He was off his feet and in my grasp. I pulled him in closer so we were eye-to-eye and he started to weep as I held him.

'Please, Jacob. Don't kill me!'

My grip loosened slightly as I started to feel merciful. Then my imagination momentarily took over as I pictured this man and the other breaking and entering my house with their pistols un-holstered. I could see Mum and Dad barely having enough time to take in what was happening. Their eyes stared into the guns' barrels and then it was lights out! Each shot sounded like thunder to my ears. To me, it wasn't instantaneous, it was prolonged. I could hear their screams of pain, their suffering, before darkness took over.

My mind came back to the present moment. And without realising it, every muscle in my body had clenched, especially those in my hands. The man was battling to breathe, but I didn't let go, in fact, I gripped his throat even tighter. His voice became high-pitched as my hands tensed. His Adam's apple crunched; veins and arteries were being crushed which restricted his circulatory system from functioning normally and his eyes became bloodshot. His body relaxed, like a rag doll, as I felt his spine crack behind the neck and the last bit of oxygen left his body.

I let go of him and he dropped limply to the ground. As rage still surged through me, a scream left my mouth, but in my case, it was a roar.

There was the sound of sirens in the distance. Soon the place was going to be swarming with police – it was going to be a night that Newburgh would remember for a long time. I had to get out of there. I darted into the woods to get as far away from the main road as possible.

## 21

My mind was racing with thoughts and questions of what had just taken place. How was this all going to unfold? I ran through the woods to try and escape this nightmare, the two men's voices echoing their last words in my head. It was as though they were haunting me.

*'No don't.* He *doesn't want him harmed!'*

*'Please, Jacob. Don't kill me!'*

Who was this "He" and how did they know my name? I tried putting a face on this mysterious voice. I needed to solve the puzzle, but I couldn't, for the life of me, figure it out.

I was becoming more physically and mentally fatigued the deeper I ran into the woods. The sounds of the sirens were fainter now which could only mean I was a safe distance from their perimeter.

But, the police were the last of my concerns. Right now, I was more concerned about the strange weakness that was affecting me. My speed started to dissipate and my run was becoming more sluggish until eventually I came to a stop. Muscles started to pulse and throb as I fell to the ground in a convulsive heap. The sound of my bones cracking echoed through the woods and startled some birds perched on trees. I was in that place again where pain was uncomprehending and impossible to withstand.

My eyes gradually lost their focus as my anatomy's structure reverted itself back to human form. The spasms were intense and profoundly draining. The hairs on my body started to diminish and I was aware of my body becoming smaller in size as the bones of the endoskeletal structure arranged themselves. Night vision became darkness and claws became fingernails once more. It's hard for the body to completely understand what it's going through while enduring such pain. I rolled about the ground in agony as the process was coming to an end until, abruptly, the breaking of bones ceased and with it the pain.

I lay there on all fours, waiting for any hint of a transformation, but there was nothing, just a small breeze that tickled my body and the tranquil silence of the woods. I let out an anguished scream – one of sorrow, anger and relief, and then, darkness.

My eyes snapped open. They looked around only to find the tops of trees and a dark sky. I had no concept of time; I didn't know how long I'd lain there. Minutes? Hours? Or longer? The strain of the transformation I'd just endured had left a massive impact on my body. It was weak, dishevelled and groggy, like I was recovering from some sort of illness.

I took the time to study my body just to see that it was really me, and not that monstrosity. It was back to its human form but for how long? I lay there awhile in the foetal position, trying to make sense of what had happened, but it all seemed like a vivid dream. Was this a dream? Part of me was in denial. My brain simply couldn't register the whole affair; it all seemed surreal. I clenched my eyes shut, opened them and expected to be in my room, but there was no room; there was just me lying in the grass, naked and alone in the dark woods.

I struggled to my feet while holding onto a tree and tried to regain my composure. My legs were like jelly and my muscles and bones ached. Thankfully, after the little rest on the grass, the weakness was already subsiding and my equilibrium was coming back to me. As I walked, one small step at a time, the images of me killing those two men was all I could think about. I wasn't proud of what I'd done and part of me was upset.

I kept asking myself, *what would anyone else have done if they had the chance, the opportunity, to do something if one of their loved ones was killed? Would they take it?*

A cold shiver ran through my body as the temperature lowered. I needed help, and to find some sort of sanctuary. My house was completely out of the question, though Pete's house wasn't too far away. But I was deep in the woods and didn't know which direction to pursue. My only option was to double back and find the main road. At least then I'd know where I was and could just follow it.

I remained vigilant; I didn't know if the authorities were still around. If they were then it was game over.

My legs had improved; a small amount of strength had restored itself. They were able to carry me as I tried to run through the woods. It wasn't exactly a run but more of a striding out.

I went from tree-to-tree holding onto them as I moved. It wasn't long until I saw signs of the road – street lights twinkling through the trees in the distance and small houses on the opposite side. I didn't dare approach the road in case I was spotted by the police. It would seem a bit suspicious that a naked man was wandering about the woods. Instead, I walked parallel with it and remained out of sight, keeping my distance as I moved towards Pete's house now that I knew where I was.

The house was just up ahead. I took one last look behind me and saw the flickering of blue lights. I kept low in case they were moving towards me, but they appeared to be still; they'd probably cordoned off the area. I assumed they were busy with investigations and trying to keep the bad news at a minimum from prying eyes.

My stomach rumbled furiously, and I was severely dehydrated. My feet were aching from the hard surface, causing me to stop for a break. Pete's house wasn't far, but it felt like hours by the time I got there. There was a small light that I perceived through the gaps of the trees. *It has to be Pete's house.*

I followed this light and used it as a guide. I looked behind me once more to make sure I wasn't being followed. It all seemed to be safe and my passage was clear. I got up and made my move. I prayed Pete was in and hoped he could help me. After all, he was probably left with questions after the phone call.

As I got closer to the light, I could see that it was definitely Pete's house. I'd never forget his garden with the barbecue next to the back door and the shed on the left attached to the house which was full of camping gear and his bike – if he still had it. The back garden faced the quiet woods, giving it the effect of tranquillity. Lucky for me, Pete didn't have neighbours, and the house was a bungalow.

His room faced the back garden. I knelt against the wall near the door and tried to get his attention. I couldn't exactly knock and have his parents answer. It was going to be difficult and embarrassing, but there was no other way. I spotted him and waved, but he was too busy pacing his room, rubbing his hands together nervously which, I can only assume, was because of the phone call. I moved past the door and knelt at his window on the right side of the house. I reached one hand up, still keeping low, and knocked on the window.

## 22

Pete came to the window, undid the latch and pulled it upwards. He looked down and found me crouching against the wall under the windowsill. A dumbfounded expression formed on his face. 'Jacob? What the fu—'

'Please, you have to help me, Pete,' I pleaded.

He must've thought it was nothing more than a practical joke. His manner showed he was incredulous, but also amused that I was roaming around naked in his garden.

'What's happened? I tried phoning you back, but no answer,' he said while clearing a path as I climbed through.

My strength wasn't fully restored and I had difficulty climbing through the window. With a strenuous effort I finally made it and slouched to his floor, panting. I always felt relaxed in Pete's room; the wallpaper was dark-blue which didn't reflect much light from his desk lamp. The room had an odd dimness to it, but Pete liked it that way. It was also good in my case as it slightly hid my dignity.

Pete took a moment to talk; he obviously still couldn't comprehend what was happening. He left the room and came back with a blanket and handed it to me.

'Thanks,' I said feebly.

He eventually asked the main question he clearly wanted to ask, 'Why are you naked? What happened to you on the phone?'

'It's a long story,' I said, with heavy breaths. 'Do you have any clothes I can borrow?'

'My dad might have some that would fit you. I'll have a look in his wardrobe—'

'Wait, don't tell them what's happened!' I said anxiously.

'It's fine, they're not in. Mum's away for a couple of days to clear her head, and my dad is at a friend's house. They both need a break from one another.'

I sat back again feeling relieved that his parents weren't in, I felt bad for their predicament, but there were bigger things at hand. I still had the urge to tell someone; someone had to know what had happened tonight, but what could I do? And who could I tell? No one would believe me. Did I go to the authorities? Or did I bite the bullet and figure this out for myself?

*Will Pete believe me if I tell him?*

It seemed there was a connection somewhere: the two mysterious men had obviously been talking to someone who was running this show and this *someone* didn't want me harmed. Did they know what I was? Did they somehow know the thing I was going to become?

Pete came back with some clothes, but before I put them on, I asked to freshen up.

The shower was rejuvenating against my skin; I felt more refreshed knowing that the clammy sweat had left my body. After I dried myself off, I looked at the mirror; it was covered in condensation. I hesitantly put a hand against it and slowly wiped. The reflection revealed my normal self. Considering this was the first time I had stared at my reflection since the change, I was still half expecting a wolf-like creature to be staring back at me. But it was just me.

After putting on the clothes Pete gave me, I made for his room again, but before I did, I thought of how I was going to tell him what had happened. Where would I start? How would I tell him that I'd killed two men? And not to mention transformation –

where would I even start? I hoped he wasn't going to think I was a monster.

*Am I a monster?*

Pete was sitting at his computer in the corner of his room drinking a can of coke. There was one for me and two sandwiches. He was about to offer one of them, but I quickly grabbed it and wolfed it down.

'Jesus,' he said in awe. 'You must be hungry.'

'Ov o iea.'

'What?'

I swallowed the contents, 'You've no idea.'

The curtains were shut which made me more at ease; I didn't want anyone to know where I was.

Pete stared at me for a moment as I sat on his bed slurping down the coke. He managed a little smile. 'Feel better?' he said, trying to cheer me up.

'Not really.' I put the empty coke can on his desk and moved to the curtains, nervously peeking through them. This made Pete feel uneasy. I sat back on his bed and fell silent for a moment with my head down. I felt his eyes on me, waiting for an explanation. There was no other way I could explain it, so I told him the truth as accurately as possible.

Pete sat back in his chair, not knowing what to think of it. I knew it was going to be hard for him to take it in, but I sensed a bit of sadness in his expression. 'Jacob, I… I'm sorry. Your mum? Your dad?'

He took his glasses off to wipe his eyes. The only thing that seemed to register in his mind was the death of my parents. That being said, everything else appeared to be a complete fantasy to him. I couldn't say I blamed him.

'Something is happening to me, Pete. I don't know what it is, but I need to find out. I don't know what to do. When you phoned, it was happening. I felt something inside me being un-leashed. That's why I couldn't talk.'

He sat back and gathered his thoughts. 'Why don't we call the police?'

'No!' I exclaimed. 'No police.'

'But we should, it seems like the right thing to do.'

'And tell them what, exactly? "My mum and dad were killed, but I caught the killers by turning into a monster"? They won't believe me and they'll think I'm crazy.'

'Well, we have to do something. There must be a reason for all of this. Jacob, if what you say is true —'

'Of course it's true! Do you think I would make this up?'

Pete put his hand up to calm me down. 'Let me finish: *if* what you say is true then this could be a problem.'

'What do you mean?'

'Well, for example, the strange symptoms you mentioned before: heightened senses; super strength and jumping ten-foot fences. After you told me about these abilities, I thought about it so hard I tried to figure it out as it played on my mind, but the thing is, no human can do that.'

'What are you saying?'

'I don't know what I'm trying to say, but now that you've mentioned your transformation, it all adds up. These are the abilities of a werewolf.'

I became anxious, stood up and paced the room, 'Don't you think I know that.'

'Only the way you explained it seems different.'

'Different, how?'

'Well, according to the myth, people who are infected with the werewolf curse have no recollection after the transformation has taken place. But in your case, it seems your mind is still functional, meaning you're completely aware after the transformation has occurred. The problem, however, is that these two men in suits must be connected to something higher up.'

'The government?'

'I'm not sure.'

'But why me?'

'The only thing I can think of is you must be important; a major discovery in the field of science. How you managed to obtain these abilities is beyond me, but it seems to be the logical explanation of why you were being hassled by those two men.'

I couldn't believe what Pete was saying, but he did have a point. After everything that had happened in the last twenty-four hours, I was convinced my predicament, to some people, would be a scientific breakthrough.

'So the big question is,' Pete continued, 'how did you obtain these abilities?'

'I… I don't know. I guess the only people who knew were the two suits and now they're dead.'

'There has to be someone that can help. Those two men were obviously working for someone.'

'Yeah. And by the sound of it, it was the strange voice on the radio.'

'Did you recognise it?' Pete asked.

I stopped pacing the room to think if I'd known the voice, but I wasn't able to make it out. 'No, I didn't recognise it at all.'

'Well, we have to find out who this person is. It seems like he knows a lot about you.'

'And how do you suppose we do that?'

'All we need is a lead. Was there anything else that seemed strange, something or someone, anything that could help us?'

I sat back on Pete's bed with my face buried in my hands. My thoughts were racing now; my mind was asking multiple questions, but it felt like I had hit a dead end. I tried to answer his question but couldn't find the words until a person in particular came to mind. 'Wait!'

'What?'

'The incident at school,' I said.

'The what?' Pete was puzzled. Obviously, I hadn't seen him to tell him of my encounter with the strange man in the toilets, and he wouldn't have heard about it.

'There was a man at school today, he spoke to me in the toilets and I had to stay behind after school hours to talk to the police.'

He stared at me open-mouthed. 'What did he want?'

'He said he was the brother of my real dad.'

'Shit. What else did he say?'

'Well, he knew about my symptoms; he was very accurate as he mentioned them. And he said...' I drifted off for a moment, thinking about the last thing he said before he ran off.

Pete was still waiting for me to continue, 'Jacob?'

He broke my train of thought. 'He said I was going to become something powerful.'

There was a momentary pause between us. We'd just connected one of the dots and Pete was the one to speak of it first.

'There you go. This man seems to know a lot about you, too. Therefore, he seems to be your lead. If only we could find him. Do you know his name?'

'His name? Ah, shit, I can't remember.' I closed my eyes and began to concentrate as hard as I could to try and remember the name.

*His name. His name.*

Finally, it came to me. I opened my eyes, looked up at Pete and spoke the name on the tip of my tongue. 'Gary Macleod!'

## 23

'Gary Macleod?' Pete asked.

'Yes. He said his name was Gary Macleod.'

'Right, now we know his name, all we have to do is find him.'

'How?'

'Oh, that's easy.' Pete turned around to face his computer, switched it on and a blue screen came up on the monitor. He was good with computers and computers were good with him; he seemed to know the right things to type in. And he was a quick learner. If anyone needed help with computers, Pete was the man to see. He cleaned his glasses with his T-shirt, put them on and started to type, his fingers pressing the keys rapidly.

'What are you doing?' I asked.

'Technology is getting more advanced these days, Jacob. You can find almost anything on the Internet, including biological ancestry. All you need is a name and basically take it from there.

'Sounds kind of scary.'

'Everything's done on the web; it's a useful tool,' he said while typing in different websites.

After a while of hearing nothing but fingertips hitting a keyboard, he finally spoke. 'Okay, I think I found something. There's a lot of sites out there that you have to pay for, but this one seems to be fine. I can find pictures, names and some addresses.'

'Let's have a look.' The screen's homepage showed a description of how it worked. It was simple really: all I had to do was type a specific name in the search bar and it would come up with the number of people of that same name. Pete moved off his chair so I could take over. I sat down and found myself staring at the search bar. I typed in "Gary Macleod" and the page changed to a list of a few people of the same name from different places in Scotland.

I clicked on one name and it came up with a photo – not the man I was looking for. The second photo depicted a South African man. I moved the cursor down to the next name and clicked.

'I think I found him,' I said excitedly.

Pete quickly approached and viewed the screen over my shoulder. We both studied the profile.

There he was: Mr Gary Macleod, 18 Board Place, Dunkeld.

'At least we have his address now,' I said. His identity information mentioned he was a scientist working in the field of medical biology. It also stated that his contract had been terminated due to mental instability.

*Mental instability?*

Maybe he was really crazy, but that still didn't explain how he knew so much about me.

'I know where that is,' Pete said, pointing to the address.

'You do?'

'Yeah. It's basically right next to Craigvinean forest. I usually go with my mum and dad for walks, and we see it when we pass through. It's just a small village with only few cottages. I've seen the sign for it, so it should be easy to find.'

We scrolled through Gary's profile to see if there was anything else that could help us. He looked better in his photo than he did now: well-shaven, his hair sitting neatly on his head and his facial expression was that of a professional business man. It was obvious the photo had been taken before things went wrong for him.

'Are you sure that's him?' Pete asked.

'I'm positive.'

'All right, let's have a look at his relatives.' Pete scrolled down to the details of his profile: there was the name of a spouse, but next to it revealed that he was recently divorced. He had no children and one brother named Terry Macleod. The name was highlighted so Pete clicked it… no photo came up. 'Uh, that's weird,' he said.

'Maybe it doesn't have his details.'

'If I'm not mistaken, usually these sites are quite accurate, but there's no photo, no address and no phone number; there's only a name. You said Gary told you that you were in danger?'

'Yeah, from his brother.'

'Seems creepy this Terry has no details. I think this could be the man you heard talking to those two men. This could be the man you're looking for.'

'But why? What the fuck does he want from me!'

I started to get frustrated, and paced the room again. It was all making sense now. The men I killed were obviously working for this Terry Macleod – my biological dad! But why kill my family? Why not just come after me instead of testing my abilities?

'Look, Jacob, we need to take this step by step. We don't know for sure this is your man,' Pete said as he tried to calm me down.

'Well, it makes sense to me. All the pieces of the puzzle have just come together.' I sat back on the bed with my head down.

Pete was quiet for a moment then he spoke, 'Now that it makes sense to you, Jacob, I think this man you encountered in the toilets was doing you a favour; he gave you a warning.'

'What do you mean?'

'I mean this man can probably help you.'

'So what do I do?'

'The only thing you can do,' Pete placed his finger on the photo of Gary Macleod, 'go pay this man a visit.'

## 24

The night was late and Pete and I decided to get some shut-eye. He went to his bed and I settled down in the spare room. I couldn't help but reflect on the events that had taken place; it all seemed like a nightmare. I knew my sleep was going to be restless. How could someone sleep after their family had been murdered? The image of Mum and Dad kept coming back to me every time I closed my eyes. And every time I tried to wipe it from my mind, it kept etching its way through again and again. I tossed and turned and eventually got up and paced the room.

After a while, I laid back down and closed my eyes once more, but sleep did not come. Images of Mum and Dad kept coming and going. Different shadows of the two men appeared and disappeared and, of course, the creature that I'd become. I couldn't take much more and found myself punching my pillow multiple times in frustration. I stopped until I was devoid of energy, and sleep eventually took over.

Morning came; daylight started to seep its way through the small gaps in the curtains. I awoke, groggy from my bad sleep, and to find myself lying on a tear-soaked pillow.

It was a beautiful morning, but to me, it seemed surreal; everything seemed... hollow. I sat on the edge of the bed, thinking: *Mum and Dad were killed and I haven't even had the chance to mourn them.* I placed my head on my hands and started to weep, but then I stopped.

I told myself to get a grip. Told myself to stop feeling sorry for myself. *Today is going to be different. I won't let the grief take over! I'm going to find out who did this! I'm going to find out who killed my parents and avenge them.*

I'd already killed two of them who were two parts from a bigger puzzle. All I had to do was find the bigger piece and bring it down to the ground. And the bigger piece was Terry Macleod. He was the puppet master who'd given the two men the order to have my family killed. I needed to find out why, but first things first, I had to find Gary Macleod and hopefully he'd be able to help me.

The time was 09:00am, and Pete was already up; he was always an early riser. 'Morning,' he said with a faint smile as we passed in the hall. 'Thought I'd leave you to sleep considering what you've been through.'

'Thanks, Pete.'

'Anyway,' he continued, 'I'm going to make us a big healthy fry-up for breakfast. It'll be ready by the time you've freshened up.'

'Sounds good,' I said and made my way to the bathroom. I leaned against the door after locking it and broke down into tears. I eyed Pete's dad's razors. *It'll be so easy. I could do it and end it all, here and now.*

I averted my eyes from them, and shook my head to get rid of the horrible thoughts. That would've been the coward's way out. I had to be strong, especially for Mum and Dad.

The shower was refreshing. I put on the clothes Pete had given me and made my way to the kitchen. My stomach rumbled as I smelt the fry-up. Pete stood in the kitchen, frying pan in one hand and offered me a seat with the other. He was still cooking even though our plates were full of Lorne sausage, fried eggs, beans, black pudding and toast. It was a good old fry-up feast and was essential considering we had a big day ahead of us.

'What time's the bus?' I asked as I munched on the contents on my plate.

'There's one at ten-thirty.'

'Good. The sooner the better.'

'My dad's not back yet. I'll write him a note saying where we are, and leave it to him to tell Mum, just in case.'

'What are you going to say?'

'I'll say I'm at the library studying,' he said as he tossed the pan in the basin. It made a loud sizzling noise.

'They should believe that. You're always at the library.'

'I know, and that's why it's a good idea; they won't think anything of it,' he said while scoffing a Lorne sausage. 'It might buy us some time. They'll find out about what happened eventually. It's a small town.'

I was starting to have doubts about bringing Pete along for the ride after he'd said this. If anything happened to him, his parents wouldn't have a clue. He'd be written off as missing and they'd relate it to the people that had gone missing from the news. I would also never forgive myself if anything happened to him and his parents probably wouldn't forgive me either.

Later, Pete placed the note against the fridge door and put a magnet on top of it to hold it in place. 'I've got the address, so we should be able to find Gary's house in no time.'

'That's good but... eh...' I tried to find the right words to tell him in a polite way that he shouldn't come with me.

'What?' he asked, looking puzzled.

'Nothing, it's just, it's just, I don't think you should come with me.'

'Why?'

'It could be dangerous. Who knows where this path I'm about to take will lead.'

'But you need my help. You can't do this alone.'

'I don't even know if I'll be back. The police are maybe searching for me as we speak. I've already lost my family and I've killed two people. I'm not going to lose a friend, too. And I don't want you to see me as... that thing. I could be dangerous and I don't know if I can control it.'

Pete looked down at the floor and started fiddling with a loose thread on his T-shirt. It had clearly completely left his mind.

'You still don't believe me, do you?' I said.

'I don't know, it's just a little hard to take in, Jacob. But I believe what I see with my own two eyes…' he trailed off and just stood there like he was waiting for some sort of demonstration, as though I had to prove to him, there and then, I had the ability to transform my anatomy's structure.

'I don't know how it works,' was the only thing I could say.

He sighed. Clearly, he was interested in these kind of things and looking for answers, but I didn't have any. 'Hopefully Gary Macleod can help me. He seemed to know a lot when I spoke to him, but it's maybe safer if I go on my own.'

Pete spoke sincerely, 'I'm going with you to make sure *you* don't do anything stupid or worse. Sure, I don't believe you, but can you blame me? Your parents are gone and you're going on a quest while grieving. Looks to me like you need all the support you can get!'

There was no say in this; Pete had me there. If I put myself in his shoes, I would've thought the same way. I took a moment to think as he waited for an answer. I didn't have a choice. I let out a frustrated sigh. 'Well, what are we waiting for? Let's get going.'

## 25

The day was dull and dank which didn't help my mood at all. I was cautious of my surroundings, my eyes were alert and I kept looking over my shoulder to make sure we weren't followed. After last night's events I wasn't too sure of how this day was going to unfold.

We caught the ten-thirty bus to Dunkeld. I was still hesitant about bringing Pete with me; if things got out of control, I might not be able to protect him. Although, I somehow felt like a new man. Regardless if I was in human form or not, I felt a constant power surge through me. Was this strange ability I possessed a disease in a benign form? Or was it malignant? If the latter proved true, it could be problematic. There was also the possibility of it being contagious and I could be putting myself and others in harm's way. Ultimately, I had to find a cure… if there was one!

We were getting closer to our destination and I was getting anxious as I stared out the window from the back of the single-decker. Pete noticed my trepidation. 'Are you all right, Jacob?'

'Not really, I feel kind of lost. Even if this Gary can help me, what then?'

I knew he was with me for support and he was trying to help, but I thought of myself to be beyond help. 'I don't know,' was his answer.

We sat there for a quiet moment. Pete was sitting on a seat in the row on the other side of the bus. 'So... eh...'

'What?' I asked curiously.

'Eh... what's it like – last night, I mean?'

'Pete!' I exclaimed.

'I just want to know.'

'Alright.' I moved from the window and sat on the edge of my seat. Pete did the same. 'Do you really want to know?' I said, my voice low.

'Yes!'

He was more curious than ever.

'Pure ecstasy. It felt like I could take on the world. But I don't know if that was my mind playing tricks on me. Do I possess a kind of werewolf curse?'

'I told you last night that werewolves don't recall anything after the transformation.'

'Maybe. I remember helping someone trapped in their car, but they were still afraid of me. I saw the fear in his eyes.'

'Then that's good, right, you helping someone?'

'Is it? Last night I was looking for blood, but not the kind a ruthless werewolf would. I was out for retribution.'

'So you could say it was a sort of vigilantism.'

Pete did have a point. I just nodded and accepted this and our conversation was at an end.

Perth wasn't far from our location. As Pete and I enjoyed the ride, admiring the countryside, our thoughts were disturbed by a peeping horn. Pete looked in the direction of the loud noise. 'Shit, it's Jonesy!' he said.

He was right. Jonesy was in the passenger seat. One of his arms was resting in a sling and he was looking up at us with an evil glare. The twins and Paul sat in the back. The driver was unknown to me; he must've been a friend or relative of some sort. I could just make out his long dark hair and waspish look as he glared at the road. He seemed to be as crazy as the others as he was driving recklessly. He was on the wrong side of the A912 road (aka the Baiglie Straight), running parallel with the bus. The road ran for a straight two miles, give or take.

The driver swerved close to the bus then back again and repeated this a couple of times. *Jesus, what else are these guys capable of?*

'HEY, FUCK OFF, YOU CRAZY BASTARDS. YOU'RE GOING TO CAUSE AN ACCIDENT!' said the bald, obese bus driver. He peeped his horn, but this only fed the manic driver's encouragement. The driver persistently swerved left and right, nearly hitting the side of the bus as if to tease us, but they were the fools. I was sure that if there was an accident, it would be them that would suffer the most due to the weight of the bus. Pete and I kept looking up ahead to see if anything was coming.

There was!

The bus driver became anxious. My eyes reverted back to Jonesy and I signalled by pointing ahead, but his gaze was set upon us. The oncoming vehicle was about 400 yards away. Jonesy just stared with soulless eyes, but Paul, who was sitting behind him, was mouthing off and performing masturbating gesticulations.

We were pointing frantically towards the direction of the on-coming vehicle by this time, but they still didn't pay attention.

300 yards.

All we could do was brace ourselves and prepare for the worst. The bus driver was distraught. His shouts becoming a wheeze. He could've slammed on the brakes, but he was probably thinking of his passengers.

200 yards.

He peeped his horn once more and I think he flashed his full beams to give out a warning sign to the approaching vehicle.

100 yards!

The sound of horns merged together until building to a crescendo. Pete and I jumped back from the window, eyes shut as we let out screams. We waited for the catastrophic collision...

Nothing.

Nothing except the screeching of tyres.

As Pete and I gathered our composure, we both stared out the window. There was no wreckage of any kind, nothing but road where the vehicle used to be. My gaze shifted to the back of the bus as the sound of a faint engine was heard. Jonesy was behind us. His friend must've known about the approaching vehicle and slammed on the brakes and quickly moved behind the bus. Either he was a very good driver or just incredibly lucky.

Pete and I breathed a sigh of relief, but Jonesy and his friends had now speeded up and moved onto the right-hand side of the road again. They flew past us with Paul giving us a parting gift by sticking up the middle finger.

We sat back down, relieved there hadn't been an accident. 'You guys all right back there?' the bus driver asked with a quivering voice.

'We're fine,' I replied.

Pete was filled with despair, 'I guess Jonesy's out of the hospital.'

'No shit,' I looked at the car as it became smaller in the distance, 'and he's pissed off.'

## 26

Pete and I got off at a stop near a caravan park. The turn-off that would take us to Gary's house was just up ahead.

We eventually came to a quiet dirt road, but before we entered, the roaring of a horn startled us. Our eyes looked down the A9 and immediately caught sight of a speeding vehicle rushing past.

'WANKERS!' Jonesy yelled as he gave the middle finger from the open-window, then they were out of sight.

'Why are they following us?' Pete was shaking.

I stared off into the distance where the car had disappeared. They were up to something, and they knew where we were. We had to be careful. 'Let's keep moving.'

Pete had been right; there were only a few cottages – it appeared to be a farming village. The road divided itself into three directions and one of them led to Craigvinean forest.

'Are you sure this is the right place? Look at the address again,' I said.

'Trust me, I'm sure. It's this way.'

I followed Pete up the path towards the forest. We walked a few yards and came to a rusty, barely legible sign that read "BOARD PLACE WALK''.

'I guess this is it,' Pete said.

We followed a small path that took us to a single, desolate house. It looked so bleak; the garden possessed dried up foliage that spread about our feet as we walked. The grass and shrubs clearly hadn't met the blade of a lawnmower or a pair of shears for quite some time. The house itself lay just before the treeline that led into Craigvinean forest. With a good clean up the whole place could be beautiful.

Two windows regarded us like eyes as we approached the front door. The house looked deserted, but we could feel a presence.

As we walked closer, the front door opened slightly and a face peered out from the small gap. It was indistinguishable at first, but the door opened wider and the man I had met in the school toilets was staring at us.

'Hello, Jacob. I knew you'd come, sooner or later.'

Pete and I were both silent for an awkward moment until I finally asked a question. 'If you knew I'd come, I take it you know what's happening to me?'

Gary nodded. 'I assume the change has happened?'

'Bit of an understatement, don't you think? What the fuck is it?'

Gary moved his body to the side of the door, 'Maybe you should come inside.'

He waited for us to enter. I started to walk, but Pete grabbed my arm. 'I'm not so sure about this, Jacob.'

'I don't have a choice. You can go back home if you want, but I'm staying.'

He let go of my arm and I approached the front door but stopped, looking back at Pete, and waited. I knew he was the curious type.

His eyes fell on the small path leading to the main road then back to me. 'Fuck it!' he said and followed me into the house.

## 27

Pete and I stood inside a reasonably clean kitchen. Gary nervously locked his door which made us a bit uneasy. We followed him to the living room. The interior of the house was easier on the eyes than the outside: wooden foundations, chairs made of wicker and an expensive glass table that stood in the centre of the living room.

Gary sat down on a chair next to the window and indicated for us to sit on a couch opposite him. He lit up a cigarette and took a long drag.

'I must apologize if I scared you the other day, Jacob,' he said, exhaling smoke. 'I can't imagine what you're going through.'

He got up and went to the television and turned it on. The news came on and I saw my house. The word ''murdered'' that was embedded on the news slide at the bottom of the screen was unsatisfactory. My fists clenched as I saw Mum and Dad's names; I wasn't surprised to see my own, but the word "suspect" next to it fuelled my rage even more.

As soon as I knew it, I was on my feet leaping at Gary. I lifted him off his feet and pinned him against the wall while his cigarette dropped to the ground. 'Why have you done this to me? What the fuck do you want?'

'Jacob, what're you doing?' Pete shouted.

Gary was struggling to fend me off. 'Jacob, I can help you,' he said, gasping for air. I'm not your enemy. You want answers; I can give them to you. I can show you what I know.'

'Jacob,' Pete said, trying to calm me down.

My grip released, but Gary's facial expression changed as he looked into my eyes. His feet were now back on the ground. He rubbed his throat and stepped on the cigarette. 'Your irises? My God. They turned yellow. Astonishing!'

I was more preoccupied with my breathing. 'I'm sorry,' I said.

Pete stood open-mouthed, but Gary was looking at me in awe, his voice high with excitement. 'An emotional response.'

'You need to start talking,' I demanded.

'Of course. Follow me.'

Gary led us into a room that seemed to have been refurbished for laboratory purposes. There was a table in the middle which held apparatus and dirty beakers lay on their stands as though they hadn't been touched for quite some time. Paper was scattered on the desk and some was sticking out of portfolios.

'I guess it all started off with my brother,' Gary said as he closed the room's door.

'Terry Macleod?'

'Yes. My brother was a good man once: smart, rich and wealthy, but all that changed after the expedition.'

'Expedition?' Pete asked, looking interested.

He rummaged through the pile of paper on the desk and gave us a crumpled, worn out newspaper article that had the heading in block capitals:

"EXPEDITIONISTS DISCOVER STRANGE CREATURE DEEP IN THE BOWELS OF ONE OF SHETLAND'S BROCHS".

'My brother and I were inseparable. We coexisted in a world of new discoveries and our work at the Macleod Institute of Science thrived.

'You studied medical biology, right?' Pete asked.

'Yes. We developed certain drugs for illnesses such as Dementia, Parkinson's, Alzheimer's and the like. Everything was going well until that day.' Gary pointed to the newspaper article I held in my hand. 'After he found that thing, his mind changed. His methods were becoming unorthodox. He was always thinking of solutions to make this world a better place. "Curing the world" is what he'd say.'

He took out another cigarette, lit it with a shaking hand and inhaled. He sat down near the desk while creating a cloud of smoke around himself. His mind wandered off as he spoke. 'It was 1984 when the expedition took place. You see, there's a small island called Mousa, not far from the main land. It's a major tourist attraction. As soon as sightseers approached the broch, these noises occurred, causing them to flee back to the boat till, eventually, the island became isolated and desolate. Some tourists described these noises as "strange howls".

'Terry heard the news and his curiosity got the better of him, so he decided to put a team together and investigate the source of the noise. We travelled to Shetland by ferry from Aberdeen. There were five of us including myself, a fair-haired man called Charles, who had a PhD in geology and another, younger man, Norman, who studied anthropology. I had my doubts about Norman; he looked like he'd just left high school, but Terry assured me Norman's knowledge would prove to be sufficient for the trip.

'My brother and your mum also took part in the journey. Terry was more excited than the rest of us even though he didn't express it, but I knew deep down he was. He was always ambitious when it came to his work. But for me? I had my doubts; I couldn't help but feel trepidation as we came closer to our destination.'

'Why were you afraid?' I asked.

Gary shrugged his shoulders. 'Just a hunch. It's not every day you're sent out to investigate strange noises coming from a pre-historic broch.'

He stubbed out his cigarette and continued. 'The broch that stood before us was massive–over thirteen metres high. Wonder and bewilderment came to our minds as we all stood there in perplexity with our heads pointing upwards. However, our adventure was not on the surface but underneath. There was an entire honeycomb of caves under the broch and somewhere inside these caves was the source of the noises. After walking and crawling through tight spots of the cave, we found what we were looking for. It was unbelievable!'

'What did you find?' I asked.

'At first it looked like a man, but after closer inspection we realised it was something else after it raised its head and regarded us. We stopped in horror as we gazed upon a wolf-like head. It gave out a strange noise that we could only assume was the noise the townspeople knew so well.'

'What did you do?' Pete said.

'Well, after getting a good view of its entire body, I had the theory that this thing seemed similar to the Shetland folkloric legend – a legend that depicts a creature with the body of a man and the head of a wolf. I let my crew know about my thoughts, but they found it rather preposterous.'

Gary paused then sat forward on his chair and stared into the distance as he spoke. 'The creature appeared to be injured which probably explained the strange noises. I guess it was crying out for help. We brought it back for testing. Our work colleagues stared in admiration, but Terry's gaze, I noticed, was that of a dangerous obsession. His behaviour seemed different as soon as he set eyes upon the thing. He studied it with a strange fixation, his facial expression that of someone who had just solved a difficult puzzle.

'He never left the creature's side. He spent time with it, day and night, as though they both shared a special bond. He studied it, took samples of its blood and even tried to communicate with it.

'Your mum worked by his side, but even she saw a change in him. She noticed he became isolated, ignoring friends and family. She came to me looking for help; she was concerned about Terry's health and wanted me to see if I could find out what was going on inside that head of his. I tried to talk to him, but he was reluctant to even communicate with me.

'His face though… his face appeared stagnant. Soulless. The brother I knew didn't seem to be there at all. It was like his obsession with the creature had consumed his vitality.'

Gary took a moment; his sadness seemed to represent someone grieving over a lost friend or loved one, but in his case, he had lost someone, not physically but mentally. It seemed as though Terry had now gained a dangerous obsession with the creature which excluded all other relationships and also affected his mental capacity.

Gary swallowed the lump in his throat and continued with a tone of despair, his voice faltering. 'He-he just looked at me with eyes that stared through my very soul and told me if I were a true brother, I'd stick by him all the way and if I didn't agree, my career was over; he made sure of that. That was the last he and I ever spoke.'

'Are you saying he caused you to lose your job?' I said.

Gary nodded feebly.

'What kind of brother does that?' I said, completely baffled.

'Part of me wanted to leave cos things were changing around the work environment: employees were mysteriously leaving, new rules became established like certain areas being off limits and the hours were becoming longer. New staff were coming into the picture, equipped with firearms. They looked more like soldiers than scientists, but they had no sign, no insignia of any sort. That's why part of me wanted to get the hell out of there. It was becoming dangerous and I feared for my life.

'The strange-looking armed men. The areas which were off limits. I knew Terry was up to no good so I began to think he was hiding something other than the creature.

'That was it for me. I eventually quit. Months went by but I was uneasy. I tried to get back in the lab to see what he was up to and to see if I could talk to him, but I couldn't get my foot in the door.'

Gary took a massive draw from his cigarette as the past re-surfaced itself in his mind. 'Just as I was going to give up that part of my life, there was a manic knock on my door. It was your mum. She was shaking and soaking wet from the rain. Her eyes were red from what looked like the remnants of tears and she was carrying a box. She explained to me that Terry's condition had gotten worse and she was afraid for his sanity and her own life.'

Gary stood from his chair, went to a locked cabinet, opened it and brought out the box he had mentioned. 'This box contains some of Terry's research your mum managed to steal from his study. The research shows evidence of some sort of experiment he established when he found the creature.

He opened it and placed some of the contents on the desk. The contents were papers that showed what looked like parts of the anatomy in diagram form. Each piece of paper had its own unique structure and shape of a body. He placed them one-by-one on his desk, the first starting with a human-like structure. 'You see,' he continued, 'this is obviously human, but as these phases go on,' he changed to the next diagram that read "PHASE 2"', 'we see the structure has altered slightly.'

He was right. I studied the diagram and there seemed to be a slight alteration of the bones and muscles. He went through these diagrams, each one more unique than the previous, until we got to phase five. I took hold of the diagram as I recognised the final stage. It was similar to that of myself: the yellow eyes; the lupine malformations; the claws and the teeth. But the diagram depicted a more malignant type of creature. 'What is this?'

'I think Terry is creating more of these creatures he found, only this,' he pointed to the paper I held, 'is nothing like it in any way.'

It was Pete's turn to ask, 'What kind of experiment is this?'

'I'm not sure, but the whole thing is creepy. If Terry is able to create something like that,' he pointed to the diagram again, 'then who knows what else he's capable of.'

## 28

Gary rummaged inside the box again and pulled something out. 'This was your mum's.' It was a small journal of some kind which was worn out due to the passage of time. Before he continued, I asked him, 'What was her name?'

Gary smiled faintly, 'Veronica.'

It seemed as though she was the one that had appeared the most logical throughout the family.

'She was a woman with ideas,' Gary said. 'She didn't let her work get in the way of her personal life, unlike Terry – the fool! Veronica was ambitious with goals that were never achieved, dreams that never became a reality, all because of Terry and his obsession.'

'What happened to her?' I asked.

He stared into nothing as if visualizing his words, 'She was diagnosed with the early stages of Alzheimer's which was a shame. A few weeks before she gave birth to you, she called me saying she was worried for herself and the baby. Terry apparently told her it was out of the question to go to a hospital to deliver the baby. He had his own equipment for that and his own personnel.

'I didn't know if it was her mind becoming frailer due to the Alzheimer's or she was being genuine. Now, how messed up is that? A baby being born in a fucking lab like some kind of lab-rat.'

'You were there – on the day I was born?'

'Yes. I was by your mum's side as she pushed. Terry was nowhere to be seen, but I knew he was there. He had eyes everywhere in his lab, especially in the maternity room that had a one-way mirror. I knew he was behind that mirror with his observant eyes on us.

'I was surprised they allowed me to accompany Veronica considering he'd banned me from the place, but she also had authority in the lab.

'After you were born, the doctors gave her a chance to hold her newborn, but she was in a bad way, so I took the privilege and held you in my arms. As we stared into each other's eyes, the doctors started to act suspicious and tried to take you from me. I refused and they came at me. Before I had time to think, I took action and ran but not without a quick glance at Veronica. I didn't want to leave her with that lunatic but she was passed out. I took you to the hospital knowing you'd be safer there. Veronica gave you the name she so desired – the name you have today. It was sort of her last wish. I left you at the hospital with your name on a piece of paper, hoping you'd be in safer hands. It was the least I could've done for her. As for Veronica herself, I don't know what happened to her. All these years I've been asking that question over, and over again.

'I remember my parents telling me that story,' I said. 'I didn't know what to make of it.'

Gary took another puff of his cigarette, now nearly reaching its end. 'That was the last time I ever saw her. It's a shame really, she would've loved and cherished you, and that's why I stepped in. I promised myself I'd watch over you.'

'Well, so far you've done a great job,' I said sarcastically. 'I just witnessed the death of my parents. Where were you? Why didn't you do something?' anger surging through me once again.

'I didn't know that would happen, but that was all my brother, not me. I tried to explain years ago, but your foster parents wouldn't listen. You're still alive, aren't you?'

'Yeah, no thanks to this alteration. What the hell is it? What am I?'

Gary sat down on the edge of his seat. His hands interlaced with one-another and his eyes studied me, 'When did this... change occur?'

I paused for a moment and thought back to the time of the transformation. The images of my dead parents came back to me from the recesses of my mind; a mixture of sounds mentally ran its course in my head: Jonesy and the others being verbally abusive to us, and my screams as the transformation took place, combined with the pain. I couldn't describe it as I'd never experienced any-thing like it before.

'It happened as I witnessed my parents' death.'

'I see. It could be that your transformation is triggered through emotional strain.' Gary stared at me. I could tell he was fas-cinated, judging by his wide eyes. 'Tell me, what were you like af-terwards?'

'What do you mean?'

'Your anatomy's structure. What did it look like?'

'I was taller than usual and my body was like… well, like a wolf.'

'Fascinating!' he said, with curious excitement.

I was annoyed at this. 'What's so fascinating about it?'

'Well, according to legend, the individual has no recollection after the transformation has taken place.'

'That's what I said,' Pete stepped in.

'So, what's your point?'

'My point is that you were still able to think and act the way you do now after the change.'

It gave me a slight feeling of reassurance hearing it from someone else, especially from a scientist. But another scientist came to mind which made me feel uneasy. 'Is this why Terry's after me, so he can study me? Well, he can have me and whatever it is that's in me. Who knows? he might be able to cure me.'

'I'm sorry, Jacob, but I don't think it works like that. Whatever *it* is, it's a part of you.'

'Then why the fuck am I here? I came to see if you can help me. Instead, you fill me with nothing but family issues.'

'Look, that's all I know. I'm guessing the only person who can help you with the answers you seek is Terry, but I wouldn't trust him. Although,' Gary picked up the journal again and handed it to me, 'this might help you. It's details of the trip to Shetland and I think it'll shed some light on your situation.'

## 29

Gary sat back on his chair and had another puff as I carefully scrolled through the journal. The first few pages were oddly confusing; they were in the style of scientific formula and rigid structures. There were also different theories on scientific medicines. Other pages consisted of rough texts, figures and tables. I studied the theories carefully but realised they didn't relate to my predicament.

As I turned the pages, Pete noticed something. 'Wait! Go back a page.'

I went back a page.

'No. Next one. There!' Pete placed his finger upon the words "Shetland Expedition".

Veronica had written down the events of the 1984 expedition. I read it carefully. 'It feels as though our work has taken the next step…

*June 22^(nd)*

*It feels as though our work has taken the next step. How exciting! We're in Shetland investigating an unusual case of strange noises within a tower built from the Iron Age. I usually only write a small fraction of the work I've accomplished but I have an urge to write a thorough, concise report of this astonishing discovery. I know for certain that the aftermath of this expedition will have a scientific (and maybe an evolutionary) impact on the world as we know it.*

*The Shetlands is more beautiful than I anticipated. We arrived by ferry and it anchored in the town of Lerwick (the only burgh on the island). The smell of sea air hit us as soon as we set foot on land. Endless ocean stretched as far as the eye could see. It felt strange watching the people of this land go about their daily lives, ignorant that some place on this island holds a mystery. There was so much I wanted to see, but there was little time for sightseeing. Needless to say, our excitement was overwhelming, despite our exhaustion from the journey. We immediately went to our hotel we'd booked and decided to have an early night. It also gave me the opportunity to make a start on penning this down on the journal I hold.*

## June 23rd

*We couldn't have picked a better day for the expedition. The sun was at its zenith and there wasn't a cloud to be seen. My sleep was restless due to perpetual thoughts racing through my mind, and I think I speak for the others as they also had similar issues – especially Terry. He was unsettled the whole night, like a kid on Christmas morning. We'd made arrangements for a tour guide before our arrival. We needed someone who knew the island and its history. Our guide was a kind, little indigenous man with a humorous spirit and a strong Scottish accent. We introduced ourselves.*

*His name was Robert. 'Just call me Bob for short,' he would say. He told us he'd studied Gaelic and we had the privilege of hearing a few sayings from the dying language.*

*As he drove to our required destination, conversations broke out. I, on the other hand, enjoyed the ride and observed the view of the land. The place had a sense of tranquillity; endless fields of grass covered the landscape and stretched all the way back and ended at the bases of hills that overlooked the ocean. The white* cliff sides could sometimes be spotted; the waves thundered against them, causing an upwards spray. It was beautiful to look at but also unsettling.

I immediately broke out from my trance as the cacophony of voices became louder. It was Bob and Charles – they seemed to be bonding well, exchanging thoughts on the subject of the island. Bob spoke about the places of interest and gave us a brief history lesson: the extinct volcano on the peninsula of Eshaness; ancient desert sandstones sculpted over time due to fierce storms; a magnificent rock arch that he called the "giant's leg". He also mentioned the folklore of the island – the trows, fairies and strange sea creatures. Bob just laughed at these bizarre stories every time he heard them. He was very sceptical and believed in logic rather than fantasy. But I didn't dare judge him; everyone is entitled to their own opinion.

After a while of sightseeing, we were nearly at our destination now. The roads were bumpy so trying to write this down in the present tense proved to be challenging. I'll have to create a more detailed view on the subject when the situation was less awkward.

*We parked the minibus and we were now waiting for a boat to pick us up. We filled our stomachs and I had the chance to add in another entry while it was still fresh in my head.*

*The boat arrived. It was time to go.*

*A few minutes ago, Bob pointed and we looked. 'There's what you're looking for... to the right,' he said. Our eyes gazed in astonishment as we saw the round tower. The Broch of Mousa! This iron age monument was believed to have been built around 100BC. Mousa (meaning Old Norse) housed one of the biggest brochs on the island and this biggest broch holds the secret of these strange noises that have been frightening the public. There's always been stories of myths and legends, but they're just stories. That's what I believe. But I was proven wrong. As we entered the bowels of the broch and eventually laid eyes on this creature of folkloric proportions, our minds couldn't comprehend the wolf-like humanoid staring back at us. This was the legend of the Wulver.*

**June 26th**

*The last couple of days have been exciting! Actually, I can't seem to find the right words that pertain to our experience. We're now back home and our colleagues at the lab have been flabbergasted at our discovery. They were curious to see the creature, but Terry did not allow it. He made strict rules that only limited staff were able to study it. He was even uncomfortable with that. His mannerisms appeared to be odd since we got back: sudden outbursts towards staff, lack of concentration and lack of sleep. He was either in his office or in the lab with the creature itself. It was like his mind was somewhere else.*

*Speaking of which, I want to take my mind back to where I left off. Our journey was difficult due to the interior path of the broch, therefore restricting me from writing anything down. But like I mentioned before, I've created a thorough view on the subject from the notes I penned down.*

*This island of Mousa seemed like a lonely, desolate place, I thought as our boat approached its shoreline. We set foot on land, but a heavy mist seemed to descend. We could see the broch to our right in the far distance, but it became barely visible to the naked eye. It wasn't hard to find considering we roughly knew its location and the small island was flat and unpopulated. We were all in awe as we arrived at the massive round tower – it was bigger than we'd imagined.*

*We prepared our equipment but froze as the noise we'd so feared came to our ears. Looks of confusion were exchanged amongst us. Bob said something ominous that didn't help the situation, 'And there's the sound of the unknown!'*

*It was unsettling, but curiosity drove us forward. Our thirst for knowledge wanted to make the unknown known. The sound made it difficult to concentrate and it wasn't like anything we'd heard before. Some of us worked out theories, though it was more like a guessing game of what could be making those noises. It was obviously some kind of animal. Though, I begged to differ and hoped the source of the noise was something else; something unique. A new species, perhaps?*

*We walked through the gate and found ourselves standing inside a circular interior with thick inner walls that seemed to be made of drystone. Our beams from the flash lights pointed upwards and captured sight of the mist slowly swaying its way around the roof-*

*less broch.*

       *Our point of interest was a small opening in the ground.*

*We analysed its shape and form to see if it was safe to enter, but the*

*noise startled us, louder than ever. We backed away from the hole*

*and took a moment to breathe. After my paralysis from fear had de-*

*pleted, I approached the hole again. We discussed our predicament*

*and talked about whether or not it was safe to enter this opening.*

*Terry was the one who was adamant at volunteering. His obsession*

*grew stronger. He needed to solve the mystery of the noises there-*

*fore driving us to proceed. We started to feel reluctant at Terry's in-*

*vitation as he stood at the hole opening. Charles, Gary, Norman*

*and I exchanged glances and agreed to eventually follow Terry into*

*the bowels of the broch. After all, this could be a major discovery*

*or it could be just some animal that crawled through some sort of*

*cavity and maimed itself. So I carefully approached the hole after*

*Terry descended, placed my hands on the opening and entered.*

*There was a small slope, so I found myself slowly slipping down-*

*wards. For a moment, I felt dizzy then I regained my balance. Terry* notified the rest of the crew it was safe to descend. As we continued, I took the time to look at my surroundings. I was standing in some kind of large solutional cave. Stalactites pointed their sharp edges toward the ground which also corresponded with the stalagmite formation. The air density felt humid, giving off a glistening effect to the walls of the cave – probably due to the mist. Charles had mentioned that the cave is some kind of subterranean karst region formed due to the bedrock being dissolved by acid in groundwater, therefore creating openings. These openings expand throughout time and then cave systems are created. Bob had no idea this cave even existed until now; all he said was that this was new territory to him.

We jumped, the lights from our torches bouncing around the walls as the noise reverberated throughout the interior of the cave which gave it a strange echo. It was deep and monotonous, but its tone altered into what appeared to be a prolonged whine. We were closer to its source now; you could maybe say that it sounded human.

*Our path was becoming narrow, forcing us to walk in single file and the ground started to become slippery due to evaporation and we took extra care of where we were treading. As we advanced deeper, the cave was becoming larger again. Limestone scaled the walls, water droplets trickled down from the roof and the ground we stood on was becoming even more dangerous due to the moisture in the air.*

*There was another sound which clarified our judgement of whether or not we were heading in the right direction. I could sense the source of the noise was close and our excitement was overpowering, but our hopes quickly vanished as the only way forward was blocked by a weak-looking wall complete with small cracks which I guessed enabled sound from the other side to protrude through.*

*Each of us took our turns to peek through the cracks, but none of us could make anything out. For a moment we'd hit a dead-end. We rested on nearby rocks but Terry was at the wall that blocked our way. I saw anger in his eyes as the thing separating us from the noise stood before him. Charles, however, studied the wall with steady hands and figured out that our way through was easily breakable if we applied the right amount of force. Our pickaxes came in handy; we hit the crack with good accuracy – each taking turns in the process. Terry was the last to make the final blow but his strikes seemed manic. As he stood at the new opening panting, Gary and I stared at each other in bewilderment at this demeanour.*

*It was time consuming, but eventually the wall gave way and we were staring into what looked like a lava tube. Our flash lights caught sight of another cave at the other end. At least we thought it was another cave. The lava tube was a few yards long and there was a claustrophobic tightness to it. Crawling on hands and knees, we advanced through in single file once more and as soon as we knew it, we were through and we'd finally found the source of the noise!*

*We stood parallel with one another as our eyes fell upon something we couldn't comprehend. This thing was lying on its side. It raised its head and looked at us. Shortly after, it made a powerful, resonant sound, almost like a greeting or a cry for help.*

*Now, gazing upon this thing, one would think it was nothing more than your common man – a man that appeared to be suffering with hypertrichosis as the body was completely enveloped in brown fur. The head was unique; it seemed as though it shared the same similarities to that of a wolf. Its features were completely uncanny. Curious at our presence, it showed no sign of malevolence whatsoever, but we sensed an unhappiness as we stared into its yellow eyes.*

*A small fraction of daylight pierced its way through an aperture in the roof which enabled us to view this mysterious room. With the help of our flash lights, we realised the shape of the room appeared to be in circular form. Stone pillars stood erect and others were embedded in the wall. There were also sculptures in relief that portrayed the similar wolf-type humanoid creature that lay before us.*

*Norman was the first to speak and he said exactly what we were all thinking: we were standing in some kind of ancient temple. It was incredible to think that we were standing in an uncharted region while discovering some kind of new species. Judging by the condition of the temple's architecture, Charles suggested it was built way back before Jesus Christ came to prominence. How fascinating! But it was only speculation; further research was undoubtedly needed, so we decided to take photos of the whole environment for future analysis. I wanted to stay and investigate this miracle, but our primary focus was set on this wounded creature that was still eyeing us curiously, especially at Terry as he stood over the it, arms folded with a grin of satisfaction.*

*We gingerly approached the creature just in case it turned aggressive, but the thing seemed more sombre than hostile. I knelt down beside it and shone my flash light around its body. I felt its eyes on me and heard it sniff at my scent, yet I somehow had a queer sensation of comfort. It had somehow managed to sustain severe injuries: its right leg was misshapen and appeared to be swollen; it had a laceration near its knee and some minor lesions about its abdominal area.*

*The others were too nervous to touch the thing in case it lashed out or had signs of contagion. I was more concerned with the injuries. With my first aid kit at the ready, I focused on the laceration on the thing's leg. It jumped as the antiseptic made contact with the wound which startled us, but the thing did not lash out; it still maintained a calm state-of-mind after the initial pain had subsided. I patched it up, but there was nothing more that we could've done there and then. We had to get it back to the lab.*

*We wanted to move the creature by hand but didn't want to cause further injury. It seemed to have endured enough. The pathway from where we came from was too small and confined; it was too risky.*

*After a small crew discussion on how to extract the creature proved to be problematic, Terry was the one who conjured the idea of executing the plan by chopper. It seemed overzealous, but what other choice did we have? We couldn't just leave it there and it was too important to put it out of its misery. So, eventually, we all agreed to extract the creature by helicopter.*

*We radioed the Lerwick emergency helicopter service and explained our situation. We mentioned that some of us were trained in first aid just so the pilots didn't feel the need to tamper with our discovery or become frightened and flee. We had to keep this completely discreet.*

*Our plan involved the aperture on the roof. I studied it with my torch and roughly pinpointed its length and width. It seemed big enough for a human to fit through but then again, that was for a human. The rules for the creature may differ therefore leading to disaster. I hoped I was wrong.*

Norman seemed eager to go back the way we came and to locate the roof of the temple and to let the helicopter know our location. I gave him the flare gun just to be on the safe side and off he went. I guessed this opening in the roof of the temple made the creature's cries for help so reverberant and amplified throughout the island.

It wasn't long until Norman found the opening. We viewed him from below and he shouted out something about the opening in the roof being near the ocean's surface. The opening was camouflaged within a bunch of jagged rocks on the island's shore, making it difficult to see from a bird's eye view.

I prayed the aperture was going to be big enough. We waited a couple of hours then heard the humming of propellers. Norman raised the flare gun and fired. The helicopter hovered above the aperture, causing the creature to become distraught. I engaged myself in an affectionate manner and tried to comfort it by letting it know it was safe. It looked at me and gave out a small nod. I was taken aback with amazement by this; it was like it understood the exact words that left my mouth. I looked at Terry to see if he shared in my wonder, but his expression was immobile.

*The co-pilot assisted us with the extraction by lowering down a stretcher-type device attached to the fast rope. We handled the creature with care and moved it onto the stretcher. The others were still nervous, whereas I had a bit more confidence considering that the creature kept its gaze upon me, but I was still cautious at not making any sudden movements that might trigger it to snap out. I communicated by using hand gestures. I moved my hands to indicate we were going to place it on the stretcher. It looked at me then at the stretcher then back at me, seemingly curious at my hands gesticulating around the air, but somehow, I knew it caught on to what I was saying. Its entire body seemed to have gone limp which enabled us to assist it onto the stretcher. It gave out another deafening cry as we lifted, but the process was quickly over almost as soon as it began.*

*We made sure the straps were securely fastened and doubled checked the safety hook, so we could provide a safe exit. The fast rope slowly retracted which lifted the creature up towards the opening. I felt a little uneasy and thought the worst as the stretcher swung from side-to-side as it neared the roof of the temple opening. Norman steadied it by holding the rope and we breathed and felt a bit more relaxed. It just fitted through the aperture and made it to the helicopter.*

*I saw the co-pilot reach out and pull the stretcher inwards; I didn't know what he thought of the creature, but I was hoping it didn't make him uncomfortable during the flight. We saw the helicopter's side-door close and it was off. The extraction was a success. Part of our work was over. And the temple? Well, we'll have to arrange another trip for further research; all we have to work on in the meantime is photographs.*

### June 30th

*It's been a tremendously busy week for all of us. It's good to be back home, but there's still a lot of work to be done especially after discovering a unique species that we can't yet describe.*

*Norman shared his skills of expertise and theories about the creature; it seems like it's some sort of subspecies that have existed from way back about 200,000 to 300,000 years ago (around the Neanderthal period).*

*We were puzzled at its origins. Where did it come from? And why hasn't there been any hint of its existence prior to our encounter?*

*Some of the team at the lab found the creature's morphology to be… unique. A full, thorough body exam, blood tests and x-rays were undertaken to make sure its injuries were not life-threatening.*

*Another thing I noticed was that after closer analysis, the thing has a scar down its left eye. Could it have been caused by some kind of previous struggle from its past? The skeletal structure is oddly similar to a human's only the limbs are slightly longer. The arms appear longer than the legs. Obviously, we haven't seen this creature in locomotion, but we speculate that it might possess the ability to walk on all fours or its two hind legs, depending on the circumstances and would establish bipedalism for the latter. Furthermore, the thing that baffles us most is its head. We focused on the cranium structure but still can't understand the resemblance of a wolf combined with an anthropomorphic nature. Ultimately, it could be possible for the creature to possess both human and* wolf-like attributes. The former seems evident considering the hand gesticulations I performed during our encounter.

Further simple tests were performed including the wave of the hand. Simple numbers were shown indicated by the fingers and it would then respond by mimicking the individual's movements. It showed signs of cognition during these tests and their simplicity but be that as it may, these tests felt juvenile for such a creature.

We then moved forward to speech. We held up cards which depicted certain conjunctions such as ''AND'', ''BUT'', and ''IF''. We also showed it nouns that were accompanied by small illustrations like ''CAR'', ''CITY'', and ''TREE''. We made these words audible, but the creature didn't seem keen to pronounce any of them. It didn't seem to exhibit any sign of intelligent speech whatsoever.

### July 3rd

The tests have provided us with useful information. We've learnt so much from this creature's anatomy. After further research, we've figured out that it's female and that's not all; it's – or should I say *"she" – is also pregnant! Which brings me to my own situation – I am also pregnant. What are the odds of that? We find a miracle and I now await another. The staff congratulated me. Gary was more supportive than ever, but Terry... well he was still in his own world which was disheartening. All there was was a small smile that formed on the side of his mouth. I'm getting worried. Is our marriage on the brink? Does he not love me anymore? With that being on my mind, I'm also uncomfortable with another thing – the damn nausea and sickness. Furthermore, I'm forgetting things too, and my cognitive functions appear to be affected by the pregnancy.*

*I have good days and bad days. Sometimes I can't focus on someone when they're talking to me. It's usually important what they're saying but it feels as though I'm a liability.*

*It's just the symptoms, I keep telling myself.*

*I decided to push on and continue with my research to take my mind off the pregnancy. Here's what we've learnt so far. Judging by the reproductive system, these creatures appear to mate in a similar fashion as humans do. This also hints there may be more of these creatures out there, but where? Are they a rare breed? Or are they in hiding in the uncharted regions of the Earth?*

*All that aside, we were concerned after her DNA analysis. The results showed signs of some kind of virus. Not only that, it seems to share similarities to that of the parvovirus but in benign form. Terry took note of this, and experimented with the DNA that was extracted. Gary deemed it unnecessary at that time. He did have a point; it seemed too dangerous to be messing around with this creature's DNA without the right protocol, and we didn't want to have a contagion on our hands, but Terry was adamant. An argument of different opinions broke out in the room. I intervened, but it ended with an atmosphere so intense you could cut a knife through it.*

*Later that night, I wanted to speak to Gary about Terry's odd behaviour but he was nowhere to be seen in the lab. Lately, I've been finding myself spending more time here than at home. Maybe that's the problem; for all of us. I think we need to get out, have a holiday and relax for a few days. Everyone's mind seems to be working overdrive, myself included which can't be good for the baby.*

*I guessed Gary had had enough for the day and went home, so I decided to confront Terry instead. I found him in his office, looking at the photos from the expedition. I told him my opinions and views on his methods, albeit the parvovirus being my main concern. His mood was disturbingly calm; his eyes never left the photos as he objected to my issues. I was about to speak once more but he snapped and was quickly on his feet showing me the door. As I walked out his office, trying to hold the tears, it felt as though I didn't know this man I'd just previously confronted. The old Terry was never like that. He was a professional enthusiast, and was the man I loved.*

### *July 30*th

*I feel lost now. My condition has left me isolated in the lab as Terry has gone back to Shetland for further research on these strange creatures, and to prove that more of them exist. But unfortunately, I had to stay behind due to the pregnancy. Terry was concerned – he sure picked a good time to start caring. Gary was very seldom at the lab; he and Terry still had their differences.*

*There isn't much I can do except write down my thoughts in this room I call home now. I've had staff say things to me like I was supposed to remember to do something for them but I didn't recall*

*them asking. Some of them got frustrated but their mannerisms*

*changed to a more supportive way because of the pregnancy.*

*They also told me I kept asking where Terry was even*

*though they told me the previous day. Am I losing a lot of sleep? Is*

*it all related to the pregnancy?*

### *Aug 3rd*

*I woke up to find Terry sitting on the bed next to me, looking con-*

*cerned. He told me his trip was unsuccessful. They didn't find any*

*evidence of more creatures. What they did find after closer inspec-*

*tion of the temple was some kind of doorway that had no means of*

*opening. So again, I guessed they'd hit another dead end. One step*

*at a time.*

*I knew that that wasn't Terry's main concern. He wanted to*

*evaluate my condition. I became nervous at his proposal but accep-*

*ted for the safety of the baby.*

*Aug 10<sup>th</sup>*

*Terry and a few of his colleagues gave me a thorough examination. The results of the ultrasound proved to be okay. There wasn't much to see considering it was only the first trimester, but Terry and I didn't want to take the chance of missing out on checking on our baby. It was the main priority.*

*That being said, the pregnancy doesn't explain my condition. The memory loss, cognitive impairment and the slight dissociation. Terry, being the medical researcher he was, knew these symptoms well but didn't want to judge until after a biomarker evaluation.*

*It was official. The results showed signs of the onset of Alzheimer's disease.*

**Sept 20<sup>th</sup>**

I haven't written anything in this journal for weeks, as my world has been turned upside down, but I must keep my mind focused before it falters. I decided to keep my interests on the baby, use it as a focal point, but unfortunately the passages I pen down are short as my attention span isn't what it used to be. I feel the images of the discovery becoming vague as those memories slowly slip away, but every time I look at my stomach it serves as a constant reminder that I have to keep my mind focused. It'll take a lot of perseverance, but I have to try.

I still want to remember my accomplishments. As I read the events of the expedition it makes me sad that I might not get the chance to do anything like that again. I had a passion for helping the ailing – people and animals alike – but now it is my turn. I am the person that needs help; I am the person that needs reassurance.

The lab is now my home. Terry doesn't want me going anywhere unsupervised. I guess he is right, for the baby's benefit. My stomach is getting bigger, but being stuck in this lab can't be healthy at all. I am a patient at my own workplace. Perhaps I could call it a nightmare come true.

*Terry said something about a treatment, but I can't remember what he said in detail.*

<br>

### *Oct 7th*

<br>

*Terry and a couple of men I did not know – or did I? – assisted me to a small, round room. They both stood at each side of some kind of clinic chair, their hands clasped in front of them in a waiting gesture. Terry coaxed me to the chair and, after closer inspection, the chair had a hole at the base of the back cushion. It was also fitted with some kind of apparatus connected to the floor that was in line with the hole. Where the head, arms and legs would be, there were leather straps, with one for the waist.*

*Normally, fear would kick in, but being in the state of mind as I was, I couldn't comprehend the situation. I was being led blindly into the unknown.*

*The two men were firm as they got me to sit on the chair. Terry told me to relax. He was pushing buttons on a keyboard while looking at the monitor mounted on the wall. As he did this, the two men strapped me in. I eventually started to panic as they pulled the straps tight around my ankles, waist and wrists. They then put a strap over my forehead.*

*I was overwhelmed. I couldn't move. Claustrophobia set in. The chair started to move back until I was facing the ceiling. Terry stood over me and said that this was for my benefit, and what was going to happen next, was going to help me. Heal me.*

*He left my line of sight and went back to the keyboard. I heard the sound of his fingers tapping the keys and then the sound of machinery starting up. The sound came from behind me – beneath me! There was a slow, dragged out sound of something winding up, then it came to a halt. The room was quiet then a scream left me as an excruciating pain exploded in the base of my spine.*

*The pain; the trembles and the spasmodic fits that occurred were indescribable as whatever passed through my body originated from the spinal column. Overwhelmed with the experience, my body couldn't resist any longer until the room went dark.*

**Oct 14th**

*I awakened to find myself in my room with Terry sitting on the bed next to me. He told me after the procedure, I fell into a comatose state and have been lying in this bed ever since for seven days.*

*He asked how I felt. I was a little lethargic and groggy, but that appeared normal after seven days of deep slumber. However, apart from that, I felt strange – different. I had questions but didn't know how to ask. The most important one of course was the baby. Terry said it was fine. He seemed more concerned about my health.*

### Oct 20th

*As I recovered I kept asking myself: what did Terry do to me? Was it some kind of new treatment he was working on, and was I the first to experience the procedure? Again, the memory of it all served as shadows. What was most memorable was the pain. I had medical staff and specialists examine my dressing on my back and evaluate my condition. I was making good progress judging by the results. They seemed pleased but Terry just looked at me with a concentrated gaze.*

*I had permission to go outside as long as I had someone with me, albeit on the premisses. The air never smelt so good. There was a slight chill, but that didn't bother me. I was just glad to be outside again. I always enjoyed the view from Kinnoull Hill, which was where the institute was based, and the sun being out made it remarkable. I paced the gardens of the institute's grounds while gently caressing the bump on my stomach. As I enjoyed the fresh air, I didn't feel at ease as I had to be watched – Terry's wishes. He was a big man that walked the pathway surrounding the building with his hands behind his back. Carmine I think his name was. He only followed orders, nothing else. I showed him a small smile but he just stared intently.*

*As I focused on my baby, my mind turned to fear as the Alzheimer's issue crept up and wrecked my train of thoughts. I knew it was a dangerous disease, and I knew it could kill. However my story ends, I hope to leave something behind; like my research for instance. Who knows? Maybe I can leave it to my baby and he can continue where I left off.*

*As I began to become emotional due to death probably being imminent, I couldn't help thinking of a name for the baby. It is a* boy, after all. Somehow the name "Jacob" sprung to mind. I've always liked that name, and now I had the opportunity to use it.

I became excited with the naming of my baby, but my mood abruptly changed as I was blinded with a steady light. A cacophony of different sounds blasted in my ears. I screamed as my body was encumbered with the strange phenomenon attacking my senses.

Next thing I knew, I was being wheeled on a stretcher down one of the hallways. I had to keep my eyes shut and my ears covered as sight and sound became unbearable.

### Oct 31st

It's been days now, and my sight and hearing slowly adjusted itself back to normal. And yet, something feels different. The walls of the lab are thick, but I can hear the chatter from other colleagues like they are standing next to me. My sight can meticulously focus on something with extraordinary detail. My sense of smell is no exception either, I can smell the interior of my room: the walls, the air and clothing. Is it some kind of olfactory dysfunction? Are these symptoms related to the Alzheimer's?

*I told Terry about my symptoms as I was becoming appre-hensive. A couple of other scientists evaluated my condition once again. The only answer Terry and the others had was "side effects".*

### *Nov 4th*

*As I recuperated, I noticed a change within the laboratory, but not only that, I noticed a change in myself. It seemed like I didn't have a choice but to coexist with the alteration of my senses. It proved difficult, but sitting in my room in the darkness, I trained myself to adapt to the ambience. Using earplugs, I would pull them out, and if the sound got too intense, put them back in. As for my sight, I managed to obtain blindfolds and a dim light. I would change the light to different settings to adjust my eyesight's intensity. I would rinse and repeat with these little experiments until I felt able to cope with the outside world, that is if I'll ever see the outside again.*

### *Nov 14th*

*My memory and cognitive responses have progressed throughout the weeks. There appears to be a good connection associated with society. Nowadays, my concentration span has increased towards the knowledge I sought.*

*The only thing is, was this real? Was I focused, or was my mind misinterpreting information therefore establishing different realities?*

*My mind thought of one thing as I sat there in despair. The Wulver!*

*If my mind was going to be corrupted by this dreaded disease then I wanted to see the creature that may change the world one last time.*

### *Nov 23rd*

*I spoke to Terry about my plea. Surprisingly, he agreed. He sectioned off part of the lab leading to where the Wulver was kept. He dimmed the lights and had the staff leave as he didn't want me in distress due to my senses.*

*I took his arm as he assisted me down the hallway. It was nice. For a moment I thought the old Terry was back: smart, affectionate and handsome. The name of our unborn child came to mind. It seemed like the perfect moment to tell him the name I had chosen was Jacob. A small smile formed on his face. It felt as though the old Terry came back; maybe there was hope after all.*

*As we walked, he asked how I was. The subject of my heightened senses came to mind. He nodded as he listened. I was waiting for some kind of advice or for him to say "It'll get better", but he remained silent.*

*We came to a room with an interface on the right side of the door. Terry swiped his key card and the door opened sideways in two sections. The room was round with observation windows in circumference with the centre. Computers and machines blipped and beeped, their lights giving off a Christmas tree effect in the lowly lit room. It would've looked beautiful in an ordinary situation but my eyes were focused on the thing I so desired to see.*

*The Wulver was lying on a bed with electrodes strapped to her chest that monitored her heartbeat and her offspring's.*

*Electrodes were also attached to her head so the device could read the signals from her brain.*

*The beep from the heart monitor was steady, but as I approached there was a slight change in its rhythm. She stared at me with those yellow eyes. She showed the same curiosity when we first encountered each other.*

*Her mood was sombre, and yet, she seemed relieved at my presence. Terry updated me on the research of the Wulver and the parvovirus. This virus is unique, considering that the parvovirus we know is a canine disease that is extremely contagious, yet somehow this creature's immune system seems strong enough to fight the virus, therefore making it dormant.*

*After all these months, the creature showed no sign of exhibiting any communication whatsoever. Terry was disappointed with himself after he told me this.*

*As I stood at the side of the bed – Terry on the other – I had the opportunity for a closer inspection. Her bump on the stomach was about the same size as mine, but that did not interest me. What did interest me was how different she looked. She was thinner than before. Her fur was no longer smooth but now just a discoloured tousled mess. She was suffering from malnourishment.*

*I was going to take her hand without hesitation but they were strapped in. I removed the cover and her whole body was bound to the bed. I looked at Terry with disgust. He just stared back and said "precautions".*

*I don't know how or why, but my next move was irrational. I quickly undid one of the straps holding the left arm. Terry panicked and tried to stop me but the Wulver shoved him back with her free arm. He fell to the ground. The Wulver then used her free hand to rip the other strap from the bed while I focused on the ankles.*

*She quickly sat up on the bed, and we were eye-to-eye, nose-to-nose. The left hand found my shoulder and the other gently found my stomach. She closed her eyes; her ears pricked up and her heartbeat was steady. She was listening.*

*For a quick moment, it seemed like we both shared a bond. There was a calm quietness as we shared this unique connection. Her eyes opened again, the mouth started to move and out came two syllables: "Pro-tect".*

Our bond was shattered by a loud ringing. I covered my ears and saw Terry with his hand on a switch. His attention turned to the door as two armed men came in with their pistols at the ready.

The Wulver jumped off the bed and poised herself. She gave out a nasty snarl that echoed throughout the room, her arms outstretched. I knelt at the bottom of the bed still holding my ears. She saw I was incapacitated, and her outstretched arms showed she was willing to engage by any means necessary to protect me.

The Wulver noticed the armed men – noticed their weaponry, and knew these men posed a threat to her. She leaped towards them. The two men opened fire but the Wulver was too fast. She sprinted, dodged and leaped swiftly with ease. Her finesse was remarkable considering her ailment, and the pregnancy on top of that. Sadly, she wasn't fast enough.

She leaped on top of one of the armed men and pummelled him to a bloody pulp. The other managed to get a shot in that wounded her shoulder. She did not stagger; it only fuelled her rage. She went for the other, but as she landed his weapon went off again, only this time in the Wulver's stomach.

*I screamed as she lay there limp. Terry broke my grieving process as his madness was now unveiled, and I must say it was disturbing. More men came in, and Terry ordered them to take me to my room.*

### *Nov 24th*

*What have I done? Everything we'd achieved – gone! A unique specimen gone, all because of some silly notion that involved some kind of animal cruelty. Was she an animal or something else? She was unique, and now she's dead because of me. If I'd just left her alone, but seeing her in that state made me take action.*

*I don't know what's going to happen to me as I know I'm now a prisoner. Terry ordered one of his so called "guards" to stand outside my room. As for Terry, I'm not sure what he'll do to me. I believe the old Terry I once knew is now gone, consumed by his new personality. I've never been so frightened and alone. The only person who can help is Gary. I have to find him.*

### *Nov 25th*

*I fear this will be my last entry as I plan a means of escape. I have to find Gary and give him the evidence I've penned on these pages. Terry has planned something – something bigger than the Wulver!*

*The parvovirus may be in dormant form, but if experimented in an unorthodox manner then that could be problematic and could lead to an outbreak with pandemic proportions.*

*As a high member of the institute I still have clearance – at least I hope I do. I don't seem to recognise any of the staff anymore, and that isn't because of the Alzheimers. Am I delirious or is it survival instincts? I'm not sure if the treatment Terry administered helped my Alzheimers. All I know is that these side effects I am experiencing are unique. I've started to control the intensity of my heightened senses. I believe it not to be side effects, but some kind of altered ability.*

*Whatever the situation, I have to try and escape. I have to warn Gary or else I fear I may suffer the same fate as the Wulver.*

## 30

I closed the journal and gave it back to Gary. I could tell by the look on his face he wanted me to say something. 'So this creature you found is the cause of all of this.'

Gary nodded.

'What about the parvovirus? Is Jacob infected?' Pete asked.

'He could well be. I don't know for sure.'

Whatever Terry administered into Veronica's system, it somehow affected me. Was it the parvovirus?

Judging by the pages in the journal, it seemed as though she'd been through hell. I couldn't help but feel sympathy as I read her words. As the journal reached its end, it seemed it was my real "mum" that shared the special bond with the Wulver, not Terry! Maybe the Wulver sensed a kind of benevolence within her. Maybe she could help me if I knew her whereabouts. She could be the one to shed some light on my transformation and the virus. All things considered, they were connected. We also shared commonalities: heightened senses! But what about the transformation? Did she suffer that kind of devastating fate as I did?

'How did she end up back at the lab?' Pete asked.

'She was convinced she was the only one to make Terry change to the way he was before. She thought giving birth to Jacob might bring him back to normality. She couldn't have been more wrong. But she was always looking for the good in people regardless of how careless they could be. I guess that was her weakness.

'Surprisingly, I got a call. It was Terry. "Veronica needs you", then he hung up before I had the chance to speak. I was nervous and a little scared as I knew what I had to do.

'I know she had clearance, and I guessed she used that to give me permission to be by her side. Maybe she convinced Terry, and he acknowledged it to put her mind at ease. But he wasn't prepared for what was going to happen next.

'You know the rest of the story,' Gary said, staring at the floor.

'So Veronica's whereabouts is unknown. I guess the only person that can help me is Terry. If I can find him then maybe there's a good chance he'll have answers, and hopefully a cure.'

Gary sighed then looked at me with despair in his eyes. 'Like I said, Terry has changed. He's not the kind of man that listens to reason now. He's dangerous!'

'I don't have a choice.' I looked down at Gary as he sat there feeling helpless. 'I'm going to find him, and you're going to help me.'

He became uneasy, 'What? But we haven't spoken in years. Besides, what makes you think he'll listen to me?'

'You know where he is and you also know the lab inside-out.'

'You're crazy, Jacob!'

Gary still sat at his desk, nodding his head, refusing to help me. 'Please, Gary. If there's a slight chance there's a cure, I'm begging you, help me! You've watched me over the years and now I actually need your help, you refuse.'

He took a moment to answer and I found myself holding my breath. He spoke in a defeated tone. 'Unbelievable. Fine, I'll help you.'

'Thank you.'

'But I warn you, this is a dangerous path you're taking, Jacob.'

'Can't be any more dangerous than what's already happened,' Pete said.

'So, where can I find him?'

'His lab is at the base of Kinnoull Hill. He'll most likely be there, but I can't guarantee anything. I haven't seen him in a long time.'

'It's a start—' I was interrupted by the sound of smashing glass and a thump against Gary's floor. It was a large stone. Voices could be heard from outside.

'Come on out, Jacob!'

The three of us glanced out the window. Jonesy stood there flicking a stone up and down with his good hand. Jesse, Paul and Frank were also present, but I couldn't see the driver from earlier. The other three mocked us but Jonesy remained silent, all calm whilst tossing the stone. I knew he was preparing to throw it; it was in his eyes.

He pushed his arm out that was resting on the sling in our direction, a reminder of what I'd done to him. 'It's not over, Jacob.

Come on out, you little shit.' He seemed more aggressive than ever. Me defeating him in the school toilets must've knocked his ego and now he wanted a rematch to prove to his friends and everyone else that he was still dominant, still in control.

Pete, Gary and I observed them from the window, but we stayed low to avoid further projectiles.

'Shit, how did they find us?' Pete asked.

'I think they've been following us since we got off the bus.'

'Friends of yours?' Gary said.

'Eh… it's a long story,' I said. I didn't want to explain my high school problems to Gary and I especially didn't want to deal with Jonesy at that moment. But they were now riled up. They shouted, swore and eventually the stone that Jonesy held came crashing through the window once again, creating an even bigger hole.

'You little bastards!' Gary said while Jonesy picked up another stone and poised himself to throw for a third time.

'We can do this all day, Jacob. We know you're in there.'

Gary started to feel uneasy, 'These guys are going to trash my house. Whatever you did to them, I think you need to sort it right now.'

He was right – I had to face the music once more – after all, it was me they wanted.

'What do we do, Jacob, what do we do?' Pete said, chewing his lip.

'Calm down.' I looked around to see if I could come up with an idea. 'I have a plan. Gary, do you think you can distract them as we make a run for it through the back door?'

'Sure, I don't see why not, but that won't make a difference. They'll still see you running out from the back of the house.'

'I'm aware of that, but that's the only way out we've got. How fast are you, Pete?'

'Why?'

'Because we're going to split up. I go one way and you the other.'

'I'm not doing that. What if they catch me?' he said anxiously.

'Don't worry, I've a feeling they'll all come after me.'

Pete and I went to the back door and Gary to the front. But before any of us left, I made sure that Gary would still help me, 'We're not done. I'm coming back for your help.'

'Don't worry, I'll help you, just get these guys away from my damn house.'

'I'll try,' I said and left through the back door with Pete.

We stood outside with our backs against the house so Jonesy couldn't spot us. Gary's voice could be heard from the opposite side. 'Can I ask what you're doing on my property?' he said.

'Where's Jacob? We know he's in there,' Jonesy said, hostility in his voice.

'There's no one here by that name. I'm sorry, I can't be of any help—'

'Shut the fuck up,' Paul interrupted, 'you're lying. He's lying, Jonesy. We saw them.'

'You better watch your mouth, young man, or I'll come over there and teach you a lesson or two about manners and respecting other people's privacy.'

Pete and I listened to the conversation. Jonesy wasn't going to give up without a fight. There was no way out of this without them spotting us; the only option was to run. Pete knew what I was thinking and he nodded in agreement. 'We'll have to split up,' I said.

He acknowledged. 'On three?' he asked.

'On three,' I said.

He took off his glasses and gently rubbed at them and put them back on. 'Let's do this.'

Gary was now threatening to phone the police, but Jonesy still showed no concern whatsoever. I held up my hand to Pete and indicated a countdown with my fingers and whispered: 'One… two… THREE!'

We both broke off into a sprint in opposite directions, but I heard the multiple footsteps behind me.

'There he is!' Jonesy and the others ran after me en masse. At least I didn't have to worry about Pete and was able to focus on myself.

## 31

I ran a few yards down the road and the path that I took eventually led me deep into Craigvinean Forest, but I wasn't alone. I heard my chaser's footfalls behind me. I was slightly relieved they were chasing me and not Pete, but most of all, I didn't want them harming Gary either as he'd proved to be a viable asset.

The leaves high in the trees created a blanket which prevented sunlight from seeping through. As I proceeded further into the bowels of the forest, the darker it became. It also didn't help as the day was dull which made me cautious of where I was going.

I quickly looked behind me as I ran to see where they were; they were close and clearly determined to catch me. I guessed my feet crunching on the foliage was giving my position away. It was run or hide. Unfortunately, it was run for me. After the first transformation, I couldn't help notice that my body had taken on a peculiar change. The headaches seemed to have subsided and my senses seemed to be working at an enhanced rate; I assumed my sensory nervous system had altered itself pertaining to the transformation. I could feel the wind crashing against my skin as I ran; I could hear

Jonesy and the others breathing as if they were at my side; I could smell the dampness in the air and their sweat as they perspired from running. As for my eyesight, I was still running in darkness, but I remembered what Gary had said back at his house: 'It's an emotional response.' I supposed some of these abilities I could control but not the parts triggered through emotional trauma.

Dodging tree-after-tree, I stopped behind one and peeked out. I saw them standing there, panting and trying to regain their breath. Paul seemed fed up of the chase and wanted to go home, but Jonesy persisted on finding me. The rest of them started to walk away, but just as their backs were turned, I made a move I regretted. I broke into a sprint. SNAP! My feet landed on some twigs.

'There he is!' shouted Jonesy.

I forced myself to not look back. I could tell they were close behind me; I could hear the thud of their feet and their panting. Eventually their voices fanned out – they'd split up. I tried to pinpoint their location, but it was awkward due to their footfalls and voices reverberating around the forest. The idea was to pick a random direction to try and fool them.

There was a thick tree in the distance; I was almost past it when someone jumped out and we both fell to the ground. It was Paul. He gasped for breath but soon regained his strength.

'We've got you now, you little shit. HEY, GUYS, I'VE GOT HIM,' he shouted as he held a tight grip on me.

'Please, just let me go,' I pleaded. The twins swiftly approached and held my arms until eventually pinning me against a tree. Jonesy was the last to show up, his speed restricted because of his arm.

He kept coming towards me till we were face-to-face with a sinister smile, knowing he had the opportunity to do whatever he wanted to me. 'You're gonna pay for what you did in the toilets, you little cunt. Did you really think you were going to get away with this?' he said, referring to his arm.

'I had no choice.'

He threw a punch to my gut; the air rushed from my lungs. The others laughed as I tried to regain my breath. I eventually fell to my knees, but Jesse and Frank still held my arms. Jonesy pulled out his knife. At that moment, I realised there was no holding back for him; he was willing to cross the line and take it a step too far.

'Jonesy, what are you doing?' Paul said anxiously.

'What does it look like? I'm going to cut this fucker.'

'Come on. Look at him, he's done.'

'You didn't think we came all the way out here just to give him a few bruises, did you? No, no,' Jonesy knelt down to my level and caressed the blade down my cheek, 'we're going to rearrange his face.'

'Jonesy, maybe we should just—'

'Shut the fuck up, Frank, or I'll cut you, too.'

I tried to plead once more, 'Listen, you don't have to do this. We can pretend this never happened.'

'Oh, but it did, Jacob. And now we're here in the middle of nowhere with no one around and no one to help you. And after I'm done with you, I'm going to do the same to Pete.' He stood up, knife at the ready. 'Pull his head back.'

'What?' Jesse said disbelievingly.

'Pull his fucking head back,' Jonesy pointed the tip of the blade towards Jesse's face.

'Jonesy, please. Don't do this.' I felt a hand gripping my hair and my head was pulled back, exposing my throat. I feared the worst and clamped my eyes shut, then opened them again. The opaque forest was now daylight.

## Pete

I ran a few yards from Gary's house then stopped realising I was running from no one. I looked around the forest and it was quiet. I could hear the wind gently blowing the trees. There was another sound though. It was the faint sounds of our antagonists.

I had to do something to help him. I knew he probably would be able to handle himself, but two adolescents being chased by aggressive teens in the forest with no one about could lead to something disastrous. Especially dealing with someone like Jonesy.

I was still able to make out Gary's house through the treeline so I headed in that direction.

He must've heard me as I arrived. 'You little bastards don't give up, do you?' He said through the smashed window.

'It's me, Pete.'

'Oh. Sorry.' He looked around. 'Where's Jacob?'

I gazed towards the forest and past the trees. Gary knew what I was thinking.

'Well I guess we better go find him,' he said.

He came out of his house as I waited in his garden, still hearing the shouts that echoed throughout the forest. 'How do we find him?' he said while zipping up his jacket.

I gave him a humorous smile, 'Follow the shouts.'

He chuckled slightly but then stopped in his tracks. I kept walking towards the gate still talking through some kind of plan, but Gary shushed me.

'What is–'

'Shhh,' he said again. He was listening. I didn't know what to but as I stood there completely still, I, too, listened and heard it. There was a faint sound of leaves and twigs being disturbed by footfalls.

Gary took a semi-circular view of the forest and saw something I hadn't.

'Back in the house!' he yelled.

Without thinking, I did what he'd asked.

We quickly moved towards his door, but as we did there was a sound of what can only be described as a gun firing. Then some kind of projectile thwipped past us and made contact with the side wall of Gary's house. It emitted some kind of electrical discharge.

I made a foolish move by looking to see where it came from. I saw a good few figures in black that were fanned out at the treeline in the distance. They were hiding behind thick trees occasionally exposing themselves to aim down their weapons.

Shock came over me which gave this new enemy a window to take us out. Gary was standing at his doorway shouting at me to move. I eventually turned and ran towards him. His hand was out to grab mine, but just before we made contact he fell to the floor with spasms as the electrical discharge surged through his body.

I didn't know what to do. I looked behind me once more and saw the black figures advancing quickly towards me. I ran inside Gary's house, but they were coming fast. I made my way towards his back door and barged through it.

There were two more of these strange people at the back of the house. I shoved one of them out the way and sprinted towards the forest once more.

'Target's at the back of the house. I repeat, target is at the back of the house,' I heard one of them say.

Who were these people? Why were they chasing us?

I panted as I ran. My body felt like jelly due to the adrenaline. As I got to the treeline – hoping I would lose them in the forest – I felt a heavy weight clash against me. One of the men dived at me, and took me down to the ground with a thud. He rolled me onto my stomach and bound my hands behind my back then lifted me to my feet.

I got a good look at the man that now held me prisoner. His identity was concealed by a black balaclava complete with an attire of leather-padded armour. I couldn't see any insignia.

'Who are you people?' I demanded. 'You military?'

The man just shoved me. 'Move!'

He escorted me to the front of the house. Gary was slouched to the ground still feeling the effects of the discharge. He was surrounded by three of the same men that held me. One aimed a pistol at him.

'Where's the other one?' another said to the man that held me.

'He was nowhere to be seen.'

'Well, we'll just have to find him, won't we?'

'Who are you people?' I asked again. 'What do you want?'

The man who'd spoken to the one that held me approached. His eyes through the balaclava were sincere. 'Where's your friend? Where's Jacob?'

'I… I don't kn–'

A mighty roar shook the whole forest disturbing a flock of birds from the trees. All of us stood there in Gary's garden, in pure silence, looking in the direction from where the sound came from.

## 32

## Jacob

Jonesy stood back in surprise, staring at my eyes in alarm. The twins eventually let go as my body mass grew. My bones broke and reshaped themselves and my vocal cords altered, my screams becoming distorted as I laid there on my hands and knees. Then Jonesy and his goons woke up and the kicks and punches ensued. I could only feel a slight pressure against my ribs, legs and arms as my pain receptors were temporarily blocked. I felt a different sensation in one of my ribs. Jonesy's knife!

There's a certain level of how far people will go while in the face of confrontation. Are they willing to run? Or are they willing to fight? My case was certainly the latter. This change was different. It wasn't an act of instinct nor a form of reflex; it was an act of will!

After being subdued, *I* released the creature that dwelt within, *I* broke the shackles that bound it. The kicking and punching ceased after I heard my clothes being ripped from my body to expose what was once skin but now fur. My spinal column cracked itself multiple times then became elongated.

'What the fuck is going on? What's wrong with him?' one of my assailants said.

Paul was unfortunate; he was stupid enough to throw a punch I clearly saw coming. My clawed hand grasped his right wrist which stopped the impact of his punch. He was now struck with horror as my sleeve ripped away. I felt the remaining particles of my clothes fall to the ground as I took hold of his throat with my opposing hand. My skull was the final stage, and it slowly moulded itself into its lupine form. I made sure Paul got a good view as my jawline cracked and my teeth became fangs. Once more the beast that'd been haunting my dreams for years was now unleashed.

I lifted him off his feet, and let out an ear-shattering roar. My breath and a spittle of saliva sprayed his face; he was too afraid to be disgusted. Then I threw him against a tree, ending his misery. His body fell limply to the ground followed by a showering of tree bark. Frank tried to run, but I managed to take hold of his collar and whiplashed him behind me. His arms and legs flailed loosely as his body hit the ground. Jesse was severely terror-stricken and clumsily ran into a tree, knocking himself unconscious.

I viewed the knife on the ground that had slipped from my body during the transformation and immediately thought of Jonesy. I turned to face him. He was gone. I looked around the trees and sniffed the air until eventually catching his vile scent.

He'd been a thorn in my side for far too long; I wanted to kill him, but better yet, I decided to haunt him. Traumatise him. Play with his mind and break down his mental capacity. After all, if he mentioned this to anyone, who would believe him?

As my eyesight turned night into day and my hearing enhanced, it was easy to pinpoint his location. His body moved from behind trees and his footfalls were clearly distinguishable. He was panting rapidly and becoming fatigued. I caught him occasionally glancing back at me which forced him to keep moving even though his body looked as though it was at collapsing stage. I thrived on this. It was my turn to do the tormenting. There were opportunities where I could've gone for him but that just seemed too easy. It was enjoyable watching him suffer; fun to watch him being struck with fear. I stalked, roared and gave out the occasional snarl.

There was a small road beyond the treeline which indicated the forest's end. Jonesy clumsily fell, grabbing at the trees and eventually fainted on the road. He was exhausted, and his sling was hanging from his arm.

There was a shine of hope for him as two vehicles approached. Their bright lights shone on him as they slowed to a stop. I watched from behind a tree: the one in front appeared to be a black Tahoe with tinted windows and the vehicle at the back, a large odd-looking truck. It didn't seem to have any windows, apart from the front and two sides, nor a name or registration number.

The Tahoe was now stationary in front of Jonesy. The passenger door opened and someone stepped out. I couldn't see who it was; the bright lights on the truck illuminated their body, preventing me from seeing a clear visual. All I could make out was a silhouette form.

'Why, you look distressed, young man,' the stranger said.

Jonesy replied with a stutter, 'P-please. Help me.'

'Of course. Please, hop in.' The stranger opened the back door of the vehicle and Jonesy jumped in. It was strange he'd got in straight away considering he didn't know who this man was. People don't always think rationally when paralysed with fear. It was a survival instinct. I started to regret not doing anything to Jonesy when I had the chance.

Before the strange man got back in his vehicle, I heard a noise that appeared to be static, then he spoke, 'Sergeant, you may move your team in.'

'*Roger,*' a voice said.

The strange man entered the vehicle and drove off with Jonesy. It was there and then when I realised I'd heard that voice before. It was Terry Macleod. I was sure of it. I was about to make my move and pursue the Tahoe when the back doors of the odd-looking truck swung open.

## 33

Black boots pounded the ground as five men leapt from the back of the truck. Their uniform consisted of protective leather-looking pads attached to their limbs and chests and they wore balaclavas for headgear. Their uniform differed from the standard military attire and there didn't seem to be any insignia of any kind.

That's not what worried me. Sitting opposite one another in the back of the van was Gary and Pete, hands bound behind their backs. Gary eyed these men with a grudge, but Pete was shaking with fear. I became anxious and nearly exposed myself, trying to hold back the urge to help them. I thought better of it and laid low to plan my next move.

Each soldier stood in formation and faced the forest. Two of them were equipped with large rifles with a spear inserted into the muzzle and a coiled-up rope hung on the side. The others gripped sub-machine guns with laser sights and small torches attached to them to enable better accuracy in the darkness.

They checked their gear and weaponry and gave themselves a thumbs up signifying that they were ready. Their weapons had been made for one purpose: to hunt a large animal, and that large animal was me!

I can no doubt say that the situation with Jonesy was over, but I was faced with a new threat; a threat that was armed, hostile and deadly.

A man with a big stature jumped out of the passenger side of the truck; his uniform looked more supreme and unique than the others, and he wasn't wearing a balaclava. He was bald with a determined face. A powerful jawline clenched as he scanned the area. He was equipped with an odd-looking firearm with a large muzzle; the chamber seemed to be illuminated in blue. 'All right, men, you've all been briefed. You know the MO. Capture. Don't kill. Understood?'

'YES, SIR!'

'Move out.'

This man must've been their commanding officer; he was running the show now. These men were hunting me, but why? What did they want? Were these the soldiers Gary had mentioned. I could only assume they were linked to Terry and they wanted me alive so he could study me and my abilities and probably keep me locked in a lab for the rest of my life. But I couldn't let that happen.

The so called "soldiers" fanned out and came in my direction. I had to move fast, however, even though these men were hunting me, I couldn't help but focus my attention on Pete and Gary. The commanding officer closed the back doors of the truck and my focus reverted back to the big man. If I could get to him, hopefully he could provide me with the answers I needed. Though, I knew it was going to be awkward to communicate given I was in the form of the beast.

The combatants advanced in my direction with their guns at the ready. They searched with anticipation, carefully scanning behind trees and giving each other hand signals.

One of them slowly came in my direction as I hid behind a tree. His torch searched the area until it landed on my face. His eyes opened wide. My position was compromised!

'TARGET ACQUIRED,' he shouted.

Then all hell broke loose. Multiple weapons were fired and echoed around the forest, bullets penetrating the trees as I sprinted past. I had to take these men out one-by-one. The first was the one that had spotted me; his gun was spewing out bullets like there was no tomorrow. Bullets thwipped their way past me as I swiftly moved.

I ran in a semi-circle fashion using the trees for cover, gaining on the combatant; he yelled with fright as he saw me approach with great speed. He kept firing and I kept charging. My arm extended and caught him by the throat. He choked and writhed around just before I smacked his body to the ground like a rag doll, breaking his neck in the process.

Before I had time to move, a sharp shooting pain hit my shoulder. I turned and saw the remaining combatants approaching with their weapons raised. My attention focused on the trees once more as bullets continued to spray the air. I hid for a moment and contemplated my next move. It was too risky taking them all head on.

They walked in unison as they slowly got closer to the tree I was hid behind, and that's when I looked up. The branches above me were a good size and would provide cover, giving me the higher ground and the opportunity to get the drop on them.

I placed my hands on the tree and dug my claws into the bark, climbing without effort. As soon as I knew it, I was on a thick branch lying down in a prone position. By looking around, I could see they'd lost visual after searching behind the tree. They looked up but still couldn't find me.

'Do you have him in your sights?' one said.

'Negative.'

'Shit. Keep your eyes open.'

Now it was confirmed they'd lost sight of me, I had the chance to make the first move, but I had to remain cautious; I needed to take them out one-by-one without alerting the others.

They fanned out and one of them walked underneath the branch I laid on. I remained still, quiet. I poised myself to get ready for the leap. He looked left, right and then clearly had a suspicious thought that something was lurking above. His gun raised upwards, but before he had time to call out, I landed on him with a devastating stomp. He struggled and screamed as I pummelled his face and body until it was a bloody heap.

Another combatant was approaching. I jumped back onto the branch I'd previously occupied and watched him as he reported the dead body.

'MAN DOWN, MAN DOWN. Requesting to fall back, over.'

'*Negative, soldier. Your orders are to incapacitate and extract, over and out,*' the voice said from the receiving end of his walkie-talkie.

The combatant became nervous and raised his gun, scrutinising his surroundings. I was getting ready for another leap, but the branch bent slightly giving off a small creak that seemed loud in the quiet forest. He quickly looked up. His eyes met mine. 'Holy shit,' he exclaimed, followed by the subsequent bursts of his firearm. 'He's in the trees. He's in the trees,' he yelled to his other comrades.

As I jumped from tree-to-tree, branch-to-branch, I saw the others coming to the panicked combatant's aid. Their guns fired manically as I swiftly moved. The forest lit up with flashes of perpetual light that emanated from their firearms. Unfortunately, their bullets destroyed one of the branches as I landed on it. I fell to the ground and the thick branch fell with me. At that point, I had no choice but to take them head on.

I quickly got to my feet, took hold of the branch and sprinted towards the gun-crazed men. I swung it round and it struck one to the chest. The branch exploded into splinters. The man fell to the ground but was still alive.

The bullets continued to hit me which fuelled my rage. I gave out a roar, picked up the nearly-dead man from the ground and held him in front of me to shield me from the oncoming bullets. The body protected my vital organs, but it wasn't going to last.

'Hold your fire. Hold your fire,' one said as they quickly realised they were shooting one of their own.

With the body still in my grasp, I threw it and it landed on one of the combatants while the other continued to shoot at me. I grabbed his arms. We fought for a moment, our arms moving in an arch-like fashion as his gun spewed out its bullets. After a momentary struggle, he eventually dropped his weapon. The final blow was my fist making contact with his chest. His body flew a few feet in front of me.

Before I had time to finish him off, I felt an excruciating pain shoot through my arm. I looked and saw the head of a large spear impaled through it. I tried to remove it, but my body was pulled off balance. The combatant, who had the body on top of him, was awkwardly using the mechanism on his large rifle to reel in the rope. I went with it and charged at him. He panicked as my hand was an inch away from his face but another pain engulfed me. This time in my left leg. I swung round; the previous combatant I'd fought was also reeling in a rope. I battled to stay upright, but it was no good.

I struggled as the two of them tried to bind me with the ropes. I spun and kicked, my arms lashing about manically, trying to release the spears from my body, but the combatants came with me as I moved. They were thrown about the ground and were close to losing their grip. The spear in my leg was restricting me from gaining any balance whatsoever. The finishing blow was a sudden continuous pain throughout my spinal area. The sound of electricity sizzled, followed by a pungent smell of burning flesh. My muscles tensed and my body jittered and went through spasms as the plasma energy ran its course.

Abruptly, the electric torture ceased. I fell limply to the ground and tried to move; my body appeared to be under a spell of complete paralysis. My vision was blurred, but I was able to make out fragments. I held my hand in front of me – it was now back to its human form. I was in trouble!

A pair of boots casually walked in my direction and a face became distinctive – it was the commanding officer. 'So, this is who you really are,' he said as he studied my human form. 'I think you've had your fun for one day, Jacob.' His boot made contact with my face and then... darkness.

## 34

My eyes opened and I immediately tried to shield my face to protect it from the boot, but my arms didn't meet my face. It was nothing more than a remnant of memories. My arms were bound; I couldn't move them nor my legs. My eyesight seemed to be impaired, and I could hear the faint sounds of muffled voices. Judging by this observation, it seemed that my bodily senses were temporarily defective. The strip lights on the ceiling stung my eyes as I was wheeled through a hallway on some kind of stretcher. I struggled to keep them open, to see where I was and who was keeping me restrained, but it was no use. I had no strength, no power in my limbs. The paralysis still seemed to be in effect.

I was being wheeled through a hallway. A claustrophobic panic came over me as I struggled to move and tried to break free.

I immediately stopped in my struggles as I heard a voice. It was muffled, but to me it was still distinctive: it was the voice that had spoken to the men who killed my parents; it was the voice that had spoken to Jonesy – it was Terry Macleod! I managed to make out some words in my state of stupor. 'Relax… Jacob...'

His vague form stood at my side and he bent down to look at me with close scrutiny. I felt his eyes regarding me with fascination. I tried to speak, but no words escaped my mouth except a jumbled slur. Terry spoke again, but it wasn't directed towards me, it was towards one of his colleagues.

Again, I could only make out few words, '…get it…?'

'…Sir…'

'…Good…'

I felt a sharp stinging sensation on my left arm just under the shoulder. I struggled again for a moment, but Terry engaged in a soft-spoken manner as his hand fell on my shoulder. '…Worry… We'll… acquainted… enough…'

At that moment, I felt my eyelids becoming heavy; my efforts to keep them open failed and everything became dark once more.

## 35

I awoke only to find myself in a strange room. My vision was completely restored and my hearing appeared to be normal. My body felt slightly fatigued, but apart from that, there didn't seem to be any problems with my senses. I sat up on the bed and witnessed my own reflection staring back at me. The majority of the wall was a large mirror.

The memories from before came rushing back. I remembered what'd happened: I remembered the change; Frank, Jesse and Paul – were they dead? Had I killed them? And, there was the big game-changer, those men I'd fought in the forest. They were no doubt involved with Terry. And what happened to Jonesy?

As I sat there contemplating everything, I realised I was involuntary rubbing my left arm. I looked at it and just under the shoulder was a small round plaster. What had they done to me?

I looked around; there was a thick door to my left that had a small window in the middle. The room held general furniture: a desk and chair; a unit and a cupboard. I got out of bed and approached the unit and cupboard, hoping to find some clothes. The first drawer of the unit held underwear folded in a neat fashion. The middle drawer had two pairs of shoes and the cupboard housed T-shirts and trousers. The clothes were milky-white and not very appealing to the eye. I quickly put them on, felling like some kind of patient as I looked at my reflection. Was I?

Something odd in the right-hand corner of the room caught my eye; it looked like an ultrasound machine. This was no ordinary room, even though it was decorated with multicoloured curtains and fancy wall paper. Was this a hospital? Had someone come to my aid as I was lying unconscious in the forest? In a way, it felt like a hospital, but something was off.

I'd had enough of looking around and turned my attention to the door to see if I could find some sort of medical practitioner for assistance. There was no handle of any kind. I tried pushing and pulling. It didn't budge. I started to panic and bashed at the door. 'Hello. Is anyone there. Let me out. LET ME OUT!'

I looked out the window to see if anyone had heeded my calls, but all I saw was a vacant well-lit hallway. There were other doors similar to mine on the opposite side of the hallway and I noticed the doors all held a small key card lock. I was trapped like some kind of prisoner.

Just as I gave up banging on the door, I heard voices. Two men were walking in my direction. I quickly moved from the door and prepared myself by clenching my fists. Two heads appeared at the window then the door unlocked with a beep followed by an electric whir. Standing there was a tall muscular man. I recognised him and he recognised me; it was the commanding officer.

He entered the room first and saw that my fists were clenched. He smiled and pushed a button on a small device in his hand. I immediately fell to the ground and experienced the same excruciating sensation that had occurred during the battle in the forest. The electricity quickly subsided. 'Not so tough now, are you?' he said. He stood over me with his own fists now clenched. I knew he had a score to settle with me considering what I'd done to his men, but before he had his way with me, a voice came from behind him.

'That'll be all, Sergeant Carmine.'

Carmine moved to the side and a man with slick black hair, dressed in a black suit, approached. I immediately knew who he was; the voice and the blurry features that I'd seen earlier were clear this time. There was now a face to the name Terry Macleod.

'Hello, son,' he said. 'I believe you know who I am?'

'I know who you are,' I said, while still on the ground trying to catch my breath, 'you're Terry Macleod. The man who's been hunting me and ruined my life.'

'My dear boy, what makes you think I've been hunting you?'

I looked at him with puzzlement then at Carmine.

Terry followed my gaze. 'Oh, well, things unfortunately didn't go according to plan back in the forest. Just as I expected, you put up one hell of a fight, so I had to improvise for a worst case scenario. I had to create a device that would be reliable for your arrival here in case you were…uncooperative, let's say. There's a small device embedded in your spine, Jacob. It sends electrical currents through your whole body which restricts your unique cells from altering, therefore stopping the conversion.'

Terry nodded to Carmine, 'Sergeant, a brief demonstration, if you please.'

'With pleasure,' he said behind clenched teeth. The button on the small device was pushed once again. The electricity commenced for a couple of seconds and abruptly ceased. I rolled about the ground for those seconds as my body went into spasms. I could smell burning skin and clothes as I struggled to breathe.

Terry knelt down next to me, his manner earnest, 'You're more powerful than you think, Jacob. But you're in my domain now. So if you would kindly keep the beast in its cage, we can get on with what's really important.' Terry started to pace the room and eyed the ultrasound. 'You were born in this room. Veronica – your mum – wanted to deliver you in a hospital, but it seemed convenient that the miracle happened here. After all, I had to keep an eye on her.'

'Why? So you could study me, make me into your lab-rat?' I said coldly.

'On the contrary. Yes, you were born in a lab, but you were delivered the traditional way. I managed to pay for my own medical staff; I like to keep my work very private, as you may well know. After all, I had to keep an eye on your mum.'

'The Alzheimer's,' I said.

'Precisely.' Terry was surprised I knew this. If anything, he looked a little impressed.

'But you're conducting illegal experiments. Your brother told me, and I've seen the diagrams.'

'Of course. Gary was always a thorn in my side. That's why I've been keeping tabs on him all this time. Not to worry, he'll no longer be a problem.'

'What do you mean? Where's Pete?'

'Ah, yes. Your little friend is safe, for now.'

'Where are they?' I shouted.

'In time.'

'So, what else did my dear brother tell you?'

'He told me enough: the Shetland Islands; the Wulver and he told me about the two men you sent to stalk me. You killed my parents!' Rage started to burn inside me.

'Something I'm not proud of, but the results were extraordinary. After hearing about your certain attributes, I couldn't wait any longer. I had to see your full potential, therefore I had to concoct a plan to trigger it.'

Despair came over me. I started to grieve for my parents' deaths again and begged, 'Please, just get rid of whatever this is. I just want to be normal.'

'I've been watching you for a very long time, Jacob. After you were born, I knew you were going to be something special – something man can only dream of. Why would you want to be normal? Why not accept it and embrace it? And start off by asking the fundamental question that you've so desired to ask...'

I knew the question. I wiped the tears away, stood up and faced him, 'What am I?'

A small smile broke out on one side of his face and he walked to the door, 'Follow me.'

## 36

We left the room and entered the hallway. Carmine was behind me which made me uneasy. I didn't trust him. But Terry was going to feed me information about the fundamentals of my abilities, so I needed to listen to what he had to say.

Scientists passed by and gave me curious, fascinated looks as if they were desperate to study me and pick and prod at my body like I was their prize. We continued further until we approached what appeared to be two metal doors with two guards standing at the sides of them. These doors opened horizontally and we entered a large elevator. The control panel had only three buttons: B1, B2 and GF. Terry pushed B2 and the elevator lowered to that specific floor.

As I stood there, feeling the sensation of the lowering lift, I saw Carmine's hand in my peripheral vision. His thumb hovered the button; I could tell he was just itching to press it as his eyes were constantly on me.

Terry finally started to speak. 'For years we have been studying mental illness. Scientists have endeavoured to invent a cure for brain diseases such as dementia and Alzheimer's and so on. As you may know, a cure has not yet been found, until now.'

The elevator doors opened to another hallway but slightly thinner than the last. It consisted of a few doors on each side ending with two large ones at the end. He looked through one of the small windows in the door and indicated me to look.

Inside this room was a man sitting on a bed surrounded by padded walls and staring into nothing with his hands placed on his knees. I didn't know what the fascination was until Terry spoke with a decent enough tone, 'How are we feeling today, Mr Parker?' He pushed a button next to the door to activate the intercom.

Mr Parker looked in our direction, 'Fine, Mr Macleod.'

Terry released the button. 'These doors are thick, making it very hard to hear anything. Not exactly soundproof but near enough.'

'Heightened senses?' I asked.

'Precisely.'

'But why is he locked in this room?'

Terry sighed, 'They might seem calm and completely lucid now, but they commonly have episodes of psychotic rage.'

Abruptly, there was a bang and a scream from another room which startled me.

'Jumpy?' Carmine said with a cocky smirk on his face.

We went to the room with the screaming and peeked in. The man inside was thrashing about violently and punching the air. He ran to the small window, hit his face against it and screamed again. Dried blood was on his face, probably from previous episodes. His wounds were in the healing process, but he started to scratch at them maniacally and fresh blood began to ooze out.

'You said they. How many people do you have down here?' I asked.

'These are our preliminary subjects. As you can see, their lucidity is only temporary until they revert back to their psychotic state.'

'You said you found a cure for Alzheimer's? This doesn't look like a cure to me.'

Terry smiled, 'I'm glad you asked. Allow me to show you.'

We entered the double doors at the end of the hall and stood in a large, cold room. People in white uniforms walked to and fro. There was a small compartment-like building on our left that appeared to be built of white plaster with glass windows surrounding it. Scientists were sitting at computers inside, chatting away as others flicked through papers on a clipboard. A large console flanked our right. It looked to be of a complex type; it was like nothing I'd ever seen before. Furthermore, protruding from this machine were multiple black tubes that led deeper into the large room. My eyes followed to where these tubes ended; they appeared to be joined up to what looked like glass caskets – like some sort of cryogenics chamber.

It was hard to make out what these objects were considering the back and centre of the room were almost in darkness.

'Nocturnal,' Terry said.

'What?'

'Their eyes are sensitive to bright lights.'

I looked at him, confused.

'You've already seen our preliminary subjects: the heightened senses, the enhanced speed and strength, all this is only the beginning. This is the final stage,' he indicated to the cryogenic tanks.

Some lights came on that gave a clearer picture of what I was looking at. Frozen vapour emanated from the tanks which gave off an uneasy chill. The glass on the tanks were frozen but amidst the ice, something non-human lay dormant in its stasis form. Something watching… waiting. These bodies shared similarities to the diagrams Gary had showed me earlier.

'What are they?' I asked.

'The creature we found had the most extraordinary DNA. We spliced it with certain other species, but the mammalian proved to be sufficient.'

'Veronica, was she your first to experiment on?'

'Desperation gets the better of me, Jacob. Yes, she was the first to go through it. I couldn't stand seeing her the way she was.'

Terry frowned and rubbed the back of his neck as though stressed from the ordeal of having a loved one suffer from a mental illness.

'The Wulver communicated with her after all other tests failed. Unfortunately, it died not long after. I was furious with Veronica,' he said behind clenched teeth.

'What happened to her?' For some reason I wanted Veronica by my side even though I didn't know her – had never met her.

'Not long after your birth, she escaped using her newfound abilities, but not without stealing a bit of my research. I do miss her, and maybe it was unorthodox what I'd done, but she was the key to all of this,' Terry indicated towards the cryogenic tubes. 'She was the catalyst.

'I felt lost without her. My research was at a standstill, but we managed to cultivate the Wulver's blood. The results were astonishing as we continued our research. The subjects took on a change, mentally and physically.'

The tubes from the large terminal leading into the tanks provided these things with oxygen, keeping them well-preserved. I stared at these creatures anticipating that they'd wake up any minute. 'Are these…' I couldn't find my words.

'Yes, Jacob. These people were cured from any mental instability there is known to man. As mental illness progresses, the brain softens. But in our case, the DNA from the Wulver reconstructs the cells of an individual, causing them to revert back to lucidity, giving them a sense of clarity and cognition. However, the individual starts to take on a physical change: large bruises on the skin appear; their skeletal structures alter; muscles grow exponentially and excessive hair grows around the body.'

'So they were human?'

'Quite so.'

'But who would agree to something like this? How did you get consent?'

Terry was silent. But I figured it out as I saw a smirk form on his face.

'These are the missing people I've heard about. Why?'

'There was no future for them and I don't think the government would've been too inclined if I asked for subjects for this situation. I need live specimens.'

'You're crazy!' I wanted to leap on him; destroy him.

Terry just nodded. 'Perhaps. But I don't care what people think. So, how did we obtain this miracle cure?' Terry asked, like some kind of teacher testing a student.

'The parvovirus.'

Terry looked impressed. 'You've done your homework.'

'But I thought the virus was benign?'

'After we administered the creature's DNA into a host, we realised it acted like a vector. It possessed the virus, but had no significant effect. And that's when we established The Lupine Strain. Some of us were a bit taken aback during the subject's change, so we decided to work on this. The transformation took longer than a month to reach its full form. Obviously, they became unstable; we lost a few good men in the process and that's why we built these cryogenic tanks to prevent any other fatalities.'

I couldn't believe what he was telling me. 'Lycanthropes. You've created lycanthropes?'

'I tend not to use that name. I find it completely ludicrous. Genetically Modified Entities or GME for short. Not the best of all names, but it rolls right off the tongue. I'm a man of results rather than fashion.'

After all I'd been through, I was still in denial about the whole lycanthrope aspect. 'You seriously can't believe in all that?'

'Why not. Myths are usually based on some version of the truth.'

'You said their transformations took place within a month or so. What about me? Why am I so different?'

'You? Well, you're the next level, Jacob. You're one of a kind: the first lycanthrope to exist. These creatures are nothing compared to you. I spent years trying to perfect my work, but deep down I knew it was already accomplished – my own flesh and blood.'

'I don't understand. Why do I differ from them?'

'Your mum, Jacob.' Terry looked at his ultimate creation – me – and an expression of sorrow formed on his face. He turned and gazed upon the tanks and continued, 'It was hard watching your mum deteriorate. We tried everything, but there's only so much medicine can do. I had to push the boundaries and create my own solution for the problem.'

'The Lupine Strain?' I said.

Terry nodded in agreement. 'It seemed right at the time. I was thinking more about her health rather than the health of my un-born child. After the strain was in her system, I was overwhelmed at the success of this miracle cure: the change in her behaviour; her cognitive responses and her altered senses.'

'I don't understand. Has she also changed into one of these things?'

'No. Not that I can tell anyway. Her physical appearance remained the same.'

'How?'

'Her maternal immune system somehow formed a barrier, thus disabling any mutation from the strain. She only exhibited heightened senses and an increase in strength. That was my theory anyway.'

I nodded my head with disapproval. 'Why didn't you just stop there? You gave her a kind of new lease on life. Why create these... things?' My attention turned to the cryo tubes again as I felt them watching us.

'Have you ever achieved something but thought you could do it better, Jacob? I had the opportunity to create a myth and make it into a reality. How I wish Veronica was here by my side to witness what I've accomplished.'

'I don't think she'd be too thrilled,' I said.

Terry went silent for a moment. He seemed to be in a world of his own, probably reminiscing about his long lost love, so I turned my attention back to myself. 'How do you know so much about me?'

Terry smiled and pushed a button that activated a monitor screen anchored to one of the walls next to the large terminal. Video footage came on which showed my house in the distance. The camera seemed to be lying on the dashboard of some sort of vehicle. I saw a man approach my door. He looked scruffy. My dad opened the door and they started to speak. I saw my younger self approaching the house as Dad got angry. The man walked away and I entered. This was the first encounter between Dad and Gary. The footage ended and changed to a slightly older me on the high street of Newburgh. This footage showed the events of the BMW pursuing my every move through the town.

As I watched, Terry started to speak as though explaining the video to students in a seminar. 'It's remarkable, isn't it? Your speed and agility develops throughout your adolescence. But there was obviously more to this. As soon as I saw this footage from my two fellow employees, I became desperate. I had to see more; I had to see your full potential and that's why I had to push the boundaries. You see, Jacob, I've been watching you ever since my no-good brother took you away from me.'

The video changed only this time the camera was approaching my door and entered the house. Pistols with sound suppressors appeared at the bottom of the screen. I felt nauseous, knowing what was coming. My palms became sweaty and I clenched them as I watched.

'I couldn't wait any longer, Jacob,' Terry said. 'I knew there was something unique deep within you. So I took action and forced it out.'

My living room door opened to expose Dad on his chair and Mum on the couch. They panicked as they saw the two men with guns. No screams came; the only sound was the two guns being fired. 'NO, no.' My hands found my eyes and tears. My body went limp and I fell to the floor. A mixture of sadness and anger gripped me.

After seeing the murder of my parents take place, it sent another trigger for the beast to awaken within me. My teeth were clenched and so were my fists. Tears and drool fell to the floor; the change was now imminent.

Terry was now leaning towards me and spoke in a fascinated tone as I was on all fours. 'Do you feel it? Do you feel it,

Jacob? Do you feel it surging through your entire body? What's it like? This is what I want, Jacob. I want to help you and others harness this kind of power and change the world as we know it. Your mum gained the abilities, but you acquired the whole package. Don't feel bad for killing my two accomplices for killing your loved ones. After all, it's a natural instinct to protect the ones you love and seek retribution for the ones you've lost.'

As my body altered, I tried to grab Terry's throat, but he pushed it aside. 'Sergeant Carmine, if you please.'

Carmine pushed the button on the device sending electricity through my body once more, causing the transformation to diminish.

'Did you really think I'd let you change that easily, Jacob? I'm not that naïve,' Terry said, solemnity in his voice.

I had to stop this man regardless if he was my dad: illegal experiments; genetic abominations. What else was he capable of?

Not long after, Carmine moved closer to Terry. They talked quietly with their backs to me then Carmine walked off through the doors we'd previously came through.

Terry turned to face me, 'Look at you, a supreme being and yet, somehow, I'm in control of you.' He gave out a small laugh. He crouched next to me again and indicated to the video monitor that was still playing; it was now playing my first transformation. The two men must've placed hidden cameras, orchestrating some kind of freak show to satisfy him. It looked surreal from a different point of view.

'Look,' Terry continued. His hands took hold of my head, forcing me to watch, 'I bet you were thinking: "My God, what's happening to me? Is this a curse? A nightmare?"'

He turned his attention back towards me and I just stared at him as he still had a firm grip of my head. 'You're just dying to change, aren't you? You want to embrace the beast within and kill me where I stand, don't you? That's what differs you from them,' he pointed to the tanks again. 'You go by your primary instinct, but your mind is still intact. These creatures have no ambition, they don't care about morals.'

'Why? Why do this?' I asked.

'My dream was to create a cure for Alzheimer's, but I've developed it into something much bigger. The creation of a new species.'

## 37

As I lay there recovering, Carmine came back through the doors, but he wasn't alone. Gary and Pete were with him, held at gunpoint by two armed guards wearing the same uniform as the ones from Craigvinean Forest. They seemed unharmed, for now.

'Pete! Are you alright? How did they get you?'

Terry interrupted, 'I told you, Jacob, I've been keeping a close eye on you and Gary.'

'Didn't think you were that naive, Terry,' Gary said.

'It's good to see you too, brother.'

Pete was mesmerised by the cryo tubes that stood before us. 'Jacob. They're the victims that were kidnapped. Those things in the cryogenic tanks are the victims!'

'I know,' I said, then my gaze shifted back to Terry. '*He* told me everything.'

'Your friend and I had a little chat, Jacob – we shared and exchanged thoughts about our beliefs,' Terry said.

'We didn't share in anything. You're a monster!' I was surprised to hear Pete say something like this, especially to a man like

Terry. Maybe after all the shit he'd put up with, he now had a bit of a backbone. He didn't seem like the shy helpless boy I used to know. He'd had his own transformation.

Terry ignored Pete's remark and focused on Gary. He approached him until the two brothers were face-to-face. Terry was the first to speak, beginning with a sigh, 'You disappoint me, brother. You could've joined me in this miracle, but you decided to go against me.'

'Miracle? Is that what you'd call it? For Christ's sake, Terry, look at what you're doing; these things are abominations. What exactly do you intend to do with them?'

'Oh, you'll see,' he said under his breath. 'I need to get the full benefit of these creatures' capabilities and reliabilities. Compare them with Jacob's attributes.'

'You know that's not possible,' Gary said.

'Maybe, but after a full analysis while being fully active, I can finally see what we're missing. Jacob can change at will with his mind still intact. The GME can't and that's where we reach a dead-end.'

'But people will get hurt,' Pete stepped in.

Terry moved in front of Pete. 'You seem like a smart young man. Can't you see what I'm trying to do here? I want to see if these creatures can survive in the outside world; I want to see if they match,' Terry pointed a finger in my direction, 'your best friend's abilities. I want to prove to myself that these twelve miracles are worthy of a scientific breakthrough.' He turned his attention towards the twelve tanks that hung in mid-air and which were being held by a large metal mechanism. An emotional smile formed on his face, yet through someone else's eyes, it was the smile of a mad man.

I sat up; my body still felt weak and weary, and I could still smell burning clothes and flesh. Terry was still mesmerised, but I interrupted his hypnotic trance. 'What about a cure?'

He turned to face me with a confused expression on his face. 'I'm sorry?'

'You created the virus, so there must be a cure. A vaccine of some sort?'

'Why would you want a cure? I'd give anything to have what you've got, Jacob.'

'If you're really dedicated to your work then it should be you in those tanks and not those innocent people you abducted.'

Terry seemed taken aback. I'd hit a nerve. He replied callously, 'There is no cure! You thought you'd come here looking for a cure and instead, you've only found disappointment.'

'We can create one,' Gary said.

'Now why would we do that?'

'Because that's what we do: we find medicine for diseases. Or have you forgotten that?'

Terry outstretched his arm with an open palm, 'Does all this look like a disease?'

'If we just—'

He interrupted Gary, 'Enough! Precious time is being wasted and I'm a man that works around the clock.'

'You always have been,' Gary said coldly.

Terry replied with a blank stare then nodded to Carmine. The two guards that stood behind Gary and Pete grabbed them and two more took hold of me and dragged me to my feet.

'What the fuck are you doing?' Gary said.

Terry approached him again. 'Now I'll show you what I'm capable of. I told you a long time ago that I was done with you, and I'm a man of my word.'

We were escorted to two rooms on the right-hand side of the lab. My feet dragged along the floor; I simply couldn't hold myself up. Pete seemed to go with it, but deep down I knew he was frightened.

Gary, on the other hand, was kicking and screaming. 'TERRY, DON'T DO THIS!' The guards immediately threw him into one of the rooms and shoved Pete in afterwards.

Terry, Carmine and myself entered a small room with three walls. The two guards dumped me on the floor and left.

There was a door on the right of the room. The left-hand side didn't have a wall at all but was intact with a one-way mirror that viewed the next room which Pete and Gary occupied. The door slammed shut and Gary bashed his hands against it, demanding to be freed.

I watched them helplessly from the observation room. I was slouched on the ground with Carmine looking over me and watching my every move. Terry approached a small terminal that had a microphone sitting next to it. He clicked a button attached to it and spoke, 'Send him up.'

'*Copy that, sir,*' the voice on the other side said.

'It's time for you to be reacquainted with an old friend,' he said to me.

The room that Gary and Pete occupied seemed partially empty save for a few containers that held laboratory equipment. They were still demanding to be released by banging on the door, but their efforts stopped after hearing a mechanical noise coming from the back of the room. A small part of the floor opened in two sections and a platform appeared from within. A body in a foetal position laid there.

All eyes were on this body as it slowly moved as if it had been awakened from the sudden brightness of the room. The body stretched one limb out at a time: an arm, a leg and the rest until it leaned on one elbow and faced the scene with curiosity.

I could tell Pete and I shared the same feelings as we perceived the face of the person that stood up. An enemy that was now helpless, a leader with no followers who was now completely powerless. Jonesy took a drunken step forward and fell to the ground. His only attire was a pair of boxer shorts and he seemed to be in a state of shock. He lifted his head and saw Pete and Gary eyeing him.

'Pete?' he said faintly.

Pete cautiously took a few small steps towards him. 'Jonesy, what happened to you?'

It's not every day you would try to help someone who's been tormenting you your whole life, but if you saw your tormentor naked and dishevelled, it's certainly something that couldn't go un-noticed.

Jonesy continued his struggles to find his equilibrium, but something wasn't right.

'What's wrong with him?' I asked.

'What makes you so unique, Jacob, is that you have the ability to change at will. You've been through a lot, therefore you might think it's through emotion, but that's simply not the case. The creatures in cryogenics are different. Unfortunately, I wasn't able to perfect the transformation. Studies show that after the change is complete, there's no going back to their original human state.

'I need to know the secret, that's why I extracted your DNA when you first arrived here. And now here we are – the moment of truth! Let's observe the differentials of the creature's blood we found on the island and yours—'

A scream from Jonesy interrupted Terry's words.

## 38

Jonesy was in a state of panic and fear as his body writhed and convulsed. His cries of excruciating pain were disturbing to the ear. His body mass started to take on a hideous change; something was trying to break free from the inside-out. He had no idea what was happening to him as the monstrosity inside him slowly emerged.

An ear-snapping sound occurred, then another and another until it became a continuous bone-breaking frenzy. A mixture of blood, drool and vomit left his mouth as this process took place. His body turned into a gelatinous heap rendering him completely helpless.

It was in such a condition he shouldn't be alive. His body twitched which seemed like nothing more than a reflex, but the twitching was the bones elongating and altering. The skin, due to its gelatinous form, started to stretch and rip like pulling on a piece of bubblegum. Blood oozed from the crevices, causing his body to become submerged in a pool of crimson.

As the transformation progressed, Jonesy's face moulded and reshaped itself in an odd fashion. His epidermis seemed prosthetic; it stretched, wrinkled and eventually split. The teeth dislodged themselves from the gums and K-9-like fangs started to push their way through. As the last piece of skin fell from his body, Jonesy slithered and writhed in a boiling mass of blood and tissue.

His anatomy was now altered, the body of his former self no more. All that remained was a newborn specimen breathing in sync with its body that heaved up and down.

Everyone was in a state of awe; no one spoke a word. Pete and Gary were uneasy as they listened to the newborn's slow breathing, their backs to the door, praying someone might open it.


I hoped Jonesy – whatever he was – still had his mind intact. Was he still lucid? Or had every shred of humanity been completely diminished?

Terry's face lit up. His eyes widened and his mouth was agape. 'Magnificent! All these years of hard work and then you came along, Jacob, and look…' He pointed to the creature that was now kneeling on its hind legs. Its eyes were still shut as though they were struggling to adapt to the environment and become accustomed to the new world. 'Like I was saying,' Terry continued, 'years of hard work within the matter of moments.'

We were interrupted by banging; it was Gary and Pete. They were clearly terrified by the beast that stood before them. 'Let us out, let us out,' they shouted.

'You have to let them out of there, you have no idea what that thing is capable of,' I said.

'I need to see what it is capable of.'

'Bastard. You bastard! That's my friend and your brother in there.'

The creature opened its eyes to expose two bloodshot irises. Its dark moist nose sniffed the surroundings. The head moved round until it caught the scent of the two bodies banging and shouting at the door. Its body stood upright. The anthropomorphic posture was unsettling – human-like!

As it slowly raised its body on its hind legs, it became aware. Sinewy muscles throbbed and twitched as though it was clenching to get ready to attack.

Through Terry's eyes, it was the perfect specimen, but for others, an abomination. I knew its speed and strength were enhanced, and judging by its characteristics, it could most likely be classed as an apex predator. The lips trembled and slowly opened to show teeth and drool. A menacing grin appeared on its face which formed into a snarl then, without hesitation, it charged towards the helpless victims banging on the door.

Pete bravely leaped out of the way, but Gary was unfortunate. He was the first to taste the wrath of this beast that used to be Jonesy. It pinned him against the door and he struggled to break free while saliva sprayed on his face as the apex predator continued its snarl. It threw him to the floor with such force Gary laid there in a daze. He tried to crawl away, but there was nowhere that seemed safe. The creature swiftly moved position from its hind legs to all fours and wrapped its maw around Gary's rib. He screamed as teeth sank into his flesh and blood spewed from his mouth while punching at Jonesy's face.

It was barbaric. I couldn't take any more. Hearing the sound of screams and snarls was disturbing which fuelled my rage. I tried once again to talk to Terry – to reason with him – to try and stop this madness. 'That's your brother in there. Stop this!'

Terry made no answer. He was mesmerised by his new creation. I turned my attention towards Carmine; he was also focused on the horror taking place.

I took this as an opportunity; this was my chance. I had a temporary window which might just give me a chance to break free, but the only way to do so was to take out Carmine as he held the button. Terry said I could change at will. Right there and then I wanted to, needed to.

The creature was swinging Gary in its jaws like a dog that manically waves its toy from side-to-side. His limbs flailed in the air then started to make contact with the walls.

After the harsh beating Gary had endured, the creature threw his blood-soaked body to the floor and decided to finish the job. He was barely alive but managed to put one hand up to fend the creature off. It executed one final leap then thrashed multiple times at his face and chest as it landed on top of him. Blood sprayed after each claw made contact. Gary's body eventually laid still, but the creature kept going until he was nothing more than a disfigured mess.

Terry and Carmine were still awestruck as they watched the brother being beaten to a bloody pulp. I on the other hand was still behind them. I stood up and slowly walked towards Carmine, as he held the button in his hand. I tiptoed towards him, my arm extended to quickly grab it, but just as my hand came into contact with his, they both saw my reflection in the glass window that looked into the other room.

Carmine swiftly threw a furious punch to my face. I braced myself for another jolt of electricity; it came on suddenly. I closed my eyes and mentally spoke to the beast in the recesses of my mind. The electricity ceased, but it was only an intermission. I tried to crawl away to escape the oncoming fists and feet.

'Where are you going!' Carmine said as though he was enjoying every minute of my suffering.

The electricity came on once more until eventually hitting breaking point. It only angered the beast within, becoming agitated, furious and blood-thirsty!

I could feel it trying to emerge, trying to break its shackles and be free once more.

*Help me. Help me, please. I need you!*

Carmine laughed with glee as he watched my body slowly fry, but his facial expression changed after his eyes locked onto mine. As he became mesmerised and probably fascinated by the sudden change of form, he was struck with a kind of paralysis and his finger constantly pushed the button.

I didn't know if the device implanted in my back malfunctioned or somehow my mind was able to withstand the pain, but the electricity was now fuel for my fire. It was as though it served as some kind of catalyst. Instead of it restricting me from changing, my body somehow managed to harness its power.

Carmine's hand was in reaching distance. I took hold of it and we both became enveloped in a bubble of plasma that emanated from our bodies. The room flashed and cracked as our bodies generated a medley of high intensity snaps of lightning-like energy. This power seemed overwhelming as my bones altered themselves. The light was blinding and both our screams were fused together creating a crescendo which probably disturbed the whole laboratory.

As we were riding the lightning, I looked into Carmine's eyes as the life drained from them. I sensed a slight hint of fear as the last thing he saw was my face moulding itself into the wolf-like malformation. His body started to smell of burning flesh as smoke emanated from it, and his face eventually became a crusted black mass. The lightning supplied strength for me, but for Carmine, it signified death and decay.

The plasma-like energy dissipated. My hand – which was now claws and fur – let go of Carmine's stiff body and it fell backwards to the floor, smoke trailing from his fried carcass.

I moved round to focus on Terry, but he was gone. The bastard must've fled the scene during the transformation. However, Terry wasn't the problem. I had to rescue Pete.

My eyes caught sight of what used to be Jonesy. The creature was still wandering and sniffing, looking for its next victim. All the doors were locked, the only way through was the large window before me.

To help prevent injury, I took hold of Carmine's leg and swung his body round. It went through to the other room taking glass particles with it. His dead-weight landed on the ground with a thump, causing the creature to turn its attention towards the ruckus. Its eyes then drew upon me. The lips trembled and introduced teeth once more. Its blood-soaked body glistened with the help of Gary's blood and its sinewy muscles clenched and knotted as if ready to pounce.

As the creature poised itself, its gaze shifted to my right as if distracted. My gaze followed. Pete was behind a container, but his head was exposed. He must've been looking for a way out, but had only found two unusual creatures. He saw me and gave out a small frightened gasp and receded back to his hiding spot. Which was hopefully for the best.

My attention turned back to the creature that used to be Jonesy. History was repeating itself, only this time we were two supreme beings about to have what I hoped was the last battle to end the misery he'd inflicted on us.

We faced each other for a moment, took a few strides and abruptly broke into a sprint, leaping towards one another.

## 39

Our bodies made contact; I was shoved against the wall but managed to place one foot against it then the other and swung my whole body over his head. I landed sprawled on the ground. Jonesy turned to face me and took hold of my throat, lifting me off my feet with such strength and squeezed. His thick hands clenched and I gasped for breath. I brought up a fist and punched at his face several times. He ducked out the way and threw me across the room.

I was quickly on my feet and ready for the next attack. He gave out a massive roar and charged for me; this time, I disrupted his plan by using my shoulder to bash into him. His body crashed against the wall. My attention quickly turned to Pete to make sure he was safe. His eyes widened and his mouth opened to unleash a scream.

For that slight second I dropped my guard, Jonesy was on top of me, manically throwing heavy blows to my body as we fell to the floor. His prominent snout came in closer to my face. Teeth snapped, drool sprayed and the smell of Gary's blood was putrid. I took hold of his jaw which stopped it from clenching, but I couldn't hold it for long. With all my strength, I bent my left leg and managed to place it against his groin and pushed.

His weight was released from my body, causing him to fall backward, stunned, but only briefly. He managed to regain his wits again and charged.

We both hit the locked door, causing it to dent. His hands moved to my shoulders and he started to shove me back and forth against it. After multiple shoves, it finally gave way.

We were back in the cryogenics chamber. The men in white coats became startled after witnessing two beasts smashing through the door. They ran with haste, arms flailing with fright. One of them pushed an alarm with a trembling hand. The siren went off, causing Jonesy to look up and around, sensing the noise, looking for more prey. His eyes shifted back to me and then I was in mid-air, clashing against some equipment which fell on top of me.

Jonesy turned his attention to the fleeing scientists. The sound of the alarm and screams intermingled gave off a scene of immense panic.

Three combatants entered the lab with rifles at the ready. They were stunned for a moment as they witnessed the monster sinking its teeth into one of the scientist's jugulars. The white coat slowly became red as blood oozed from the wound and from the small gaps between Jonesy's teeth. The armed men opened fire; their bullets made contact with his body, but it only seemed to encourage his maniacal rage. He dropped the body and focused his attention on the combatants.

Their guns spoke again, but they didn't stop Jonesy on his warpath. He didn't appear to be maimed at all; the bullets were completely ineffective. He just kept going, looking for the next poor individual to slaughter.

A scream from one of the combatants was interrupted as a claw struck the side of his face. The tissue and cartilage of his skull was exposed and he fell to the ground with a gurgled cry. Jonesy took hold of one of the others and threw him across the room. His body made contact with the console that monitored the cryogenic tanks and it buckled instantly. The mechanism controlling the tanks started to move and the floor of the room opened to expose what appeared to be large tubular-like vents that were in line with the tanks above.

The tanks slowly started to lower and seemed to be a perfect fit for the vents, like a piece of puzzle being fitted into the indentation. The machine that provided the right temperature and kept the creatures preserved was deactivated which made me fear the worst. I had to destroy this chaotic beast. But how did you destroy something that powerful? Was there even a weakness?

Jonesy finished off the third combatant by throwing him into one of the vents. His body landed with a thud. Dazed as he was, his attention turned to the lowering tubes. He desperately tried to climb out as the tank that fitted the indentation slowly lowered itself.

His hands tried and nails scraped against the ground as they tried to pull him out of the vent. Down, down, it went until it crushed his body. His screams became a gurgle as the tube was now inserted, ending with a wet crunching noise. Jonesy just watched with keen eyes as his victim was annihilated then moved on to his next.

The alarm was still going and his fury caused the other scientists to flee, their screams filling the air, but there was another noise now – the noise of claw against steel.

The bellowing horror that was occurring below was a sound that overpowered all others until it slowly died away. The thought hit me: Jonesy was no longer the only problem; the creatures in the tanks were now awakened from their slumber and my guess was that Terry's plan had been to unleash them underground, giving them access to the outside world, but it was Jonesy who'd finished what Terry had started. He'd freed them from their stasis and now they were travelling underground through what I could only guess was a sewer system.

Jonesy was still destroying everything in his path; whether it was man or machine, it made no difference to him. The lab was slowly coming apart: small fires started to accumulate from the small compartment-like building near the entrance; the GMEs were loose; Terry was nowhere to be seen and Pete was hopefully still hiding in the observation room. And Jonesy… well, he was my first priority. If those other creatures in the tanks shared even some of the same characteristics as him, the outside world was in for a shock. It was going to be anarchy!

The men in white coats were no less in number; some were hiding, others were dying. Fires were spreading; a thick cloud of smoke started to form at the roof which activated the sprinklers. I couldn't let this go on. I had to do something. I stood up, gathered my strength, faced Jonesy and gave out a roar that would hopefully make him focus on me instead.

He stopped in his tracks. His body turned and his bloodshot eyes locked on to me. Water from the sprinklers splashed down our bodies. Everything happening in the lab no longer mattered. We both were stuck in a trance that seemed to block out every other aspect.

As the fire ate its way through the lab, it eventually appeared behind him, giving a sense that he'd just crawled up from the dark pits of hell. It gave the whole scene a nightmare effect that seemed almost picturesque.

He took the first step…

I took the next…

Then the charging commenced!

## 40

We clashed; claws sliced and slashed, and fists came in contact with flesh. Jonesy's arms swiftly wrapped tightly around my waist; he squeezed and lifted me off the ground. The wind was forced out of my body as the bear-hug almost reached its zenith point, but I just managed to free my right arm and brought my elbow to his face. As it struck home, he let go. His arms loosened and I was able to execute a series of devastating punches to his face before he made his next move.

As the dance of combat continued, I suffered another hit. My body fell backwards towards the entrance of the small compartments that contained computers and other lab equipment. I felt Jonesy's arms under my own and before I knew it, we both barged through the door. He flung me from left to right: windows smashed, equipment was destroyed and tables and chairs broke and shattered. Then my body was hurled through one of the small windows.

I tried to stand, but I was dazed and slouched to the ground again.

Jonesy appeared in the corner of my vision, casually approaching me with an attitude of supremacy. I didn't know if he still had possession of his mind and was power-driven by his new physical appearance, or maybe it was simply decimated and this new form only had the desire for blood – to feed. The latter seemed the most obvious.

The fire in the lab was becoming worse: smoke enveloped the roof, spreading rapidly, but Jonesy didn't seem to care. If he didn't kill both Pete and myself, the fire might.

As I gained my focus, a hand wrap itself around my leg. With his momentum, Jonesy swung me in a clockwise fashion. Eventually he let go and I landed at the entrance of the observation room. My view caught sight of his previous remains, reminding me of a hatched cocoon after the metamorphosis process. Only it was something more sinister than a butterfly that had emerged.

His footfalls were loud as they thudded towards me. I figured the only way to stop him was the element of surprise. The idea of a typical dog playing dead came to me.

I was still on the ground, lying on my stomach. Jonesy's loud, stomping feet came closer. I sensed him stand over me. His hand touched my back – probably checking to see if I was alive – and with a quick, swift move, I leaped onto his body.

We writhed and thrashed as I made my attempt to put an end to him or at least maim him for the time being by going for his eyes. My hands clung to his wolf-like head. His jaws snapped at my face making it difficult to reach the eyes. But I wasn't about to give up. Suddenly, my thumb was in the right place. I pressed down hard, penetrating his eyeball as blood oozed from the ocular socket. He gave out a bellowing sound of pain, his head tilting to one side, causing his throat to become exposed. My head came down and my teeth sunk into the taut flesh.

Jonesy was in a state of panic. He writhed and convulsed violently. I couldn't hold on any longer. My grip was eventually lost. He hurled me inside the observation room. The taste of his blood in my mouth was vile. A crimson liquid poured from his neck as he staggered, holding a hand to his left eye. He was still going strong; he still had that blood-thirsty look about him.

He made one last leap towards me as he still had the advantage. His hands wrapped themselves around my throat and he squeezed. Blood and saliva landed on me as I felt my life drain away. His snarling was mocking – a grimace that was haunting and yet I remembered a similar expression. An expression from a familiar face – a familiar tormentor. Was the real Jonesy still in there?

Just before I was on the brink of losing consciousness, a curious thing happened. His hands released their death-grip and he seemed to be disorientated. I didn't understand what was happening until he turned his back to me – there was a piece of glass protruding from his spine.

Pete stood there paralysed with fear as Jonesy faced him.

His drunkenly body moved towards the frightened Pete. Jonesy swayed and he seemed flustered, but the rage was still there. He wasn't going to mock him verbally; he wasn't going to flush his head down the toilet. No, no. He was going to mutilate him.

As the oxygen filled my lungs again, I regained focus. Jonesy's bodily movements were distorted, but he was still determined to get his hands on Pete. I was on my feet and leaped just before he attacked. I took hold of the piece of glass and executed a twisting motion.

He bellowed and his legs gave way. I continued to twist and push the piece of glass further into his spine. His body convulsed violently and his strength subsided.

The shard broke loose, but the spine was now exposed. I made a grotesque decision that I found unsettling on my part, but I had to do it.

I gripped the spine. Twisted and pulled.

It bent, cracked and snapped. I strained myself and pulled as hard as I could. Each segmented part exposed itself as it ripped the skin, causing a gaping opening as I tugged. The spine gradually came loose. The skull followed until it was completely removed from the body. Abruptly, the convulsions stopped and Jonesy's mangled body fell to the floor in a crimson heap.

I stood over his lifeless body with a mixture of emotions: pity, sadness, ecstasy. His battered carcass lay at my feet and a frustrated yet triumphant roar left my mouth.

I didn't want to kill him, but there was no other option. It was either him or me. Besides, who knew what he would do if he got to the outside world which reminded me of the GMEs. I now needed to turn my attention to them. Jonesy proved to be a chal-

lenge, but how did I fight twelve of these creatures?

## 41

The entire lab was in disarray and starting to become unstable: fire ate its way through the electrical systems, smoke billowed which caused the air to become thin and the sprinklers spewed water in vain.

Pete was curled up against the wall, eyeing me. I took a step forward, but he flinched. I didn't move and suddenly, knowing Jonesy was no longer a threat, my legs gave way and my body trembled. My anatomy was reverting back to its human state.

My screams of pain slowly became human as the bones in my head retracted themselves. The water gave off a refreshing, cathartic effect as it soaked my body.

Pete was flabbergasted as he witnessed a beast transform back into his best friend. He didn't say a word as I laid there. First, I had to cover my dignity. There was a lab coat lying on the floor just underneath a hanger. It was a bit wet, but it was better than nothing. I put it on and approached him, but my body was still weak. I could barely walk.

'Pete. It's over,' was all I could say with short breaths.

He slowly stood on his feet; I didn't know what words were going to come from him. I didn't expect him to understand. Instead, it seemed like a sense of clarity hit him and as usual, he said the most sensible thing anyone would say while facing danger, 'Let's get out of here.'

He helped me up by placing my arm around his shoulders. We took a few steps towards the door but were stopped short by his broken glasses on the ground. They must've fallen off while he was eluding Jonesy. 'Shit!' he said.

'Sorry 'bout your glasses,' I said humorously.

'It's fine, I'll just have to make do.'

We continued by exiting the observation room and made our way out of the lab. I became Pete's eyes as his vision was limited.

'We need to get to the elevator,' I shouted over the noise of fire and destruction. Our path wasn't an easy one: smoke was absorbing the oxygen, making it hard to breathe and we had to watch our step from the small flames that were scattered around the floor.

Pete slowed his pace and took a short moment to look at the mutilated bodies with disgust. He strained his eyes towards where the cryo tubes used to be and noticed the missing GMEs. 'My God, are those things loose?'

'No time. We need to keep moving!'

A deafening explosion caused us to nearly lose our footing. We quickly regained our balance and continued to move with haste, making it to the double doors and barging through them. The scientists were either gone or dead. All that remained was us and the poor patients locked in their confinement. I took a quick glance through their small windows on the door; they banged on them and their mouths moved furiously in what were clearly terrified shouts but inaudible due to the soundproof encasement.

Our vision of them became lost as we progressed through the corridor. We both felt bad for not helping, but we knew we couldn't – we didn't know how, plus they could be a danger to us and themselves.

The elevator seemed reasonably safe, but the fire wasn't diminishing in its force. I looked down the hall to where the main lab was. The entrance was now ablaze.

Pete strained his eyes to look for the button. He found it and rapidly pushed it to call the elevator, but it wasn't coming fast enough.

'COME ON,' he shouted as he punched the button with the bottom of his fist.

Another explosion assailed our ears. It rumbled under our feet which fed the flames. They were approaching fast. Pete gave up hitting the button; we were now both looking at the instrument of our deaths, but before our fate was decided, the elevator doors sprang open. We jumped in just as the fire roared its way to the doors. They closed, but the lift was full of smoke.

'Jacob, push the button that says GF.' I did what he asked and the elevator sprung to life.

We choked and prayed for fresh air. Were we ever going to make it to the surface again?

As we ascended, we felt vibrations, causing the elevator light to flicker. We didn't think we'd make it out, but the doors opened into a bright white hall.

Pete led the way on arrival. This part of the lab was completely deserted.

We stopped at the end of the hall and looked to see if any of Terry's guards were lurking in wait. Our gaze shifted from left to right, but it seemed clear.

Pete strained his eyes again, 'Come on, this way,' he said.

'How do you know?' I asked.

'We came through here on the way in. I might be partially blind but I can try and retrace my steps.'

As we passed a couple of hallways, we eventually came to a big round room that appeared to be some sort of reception. Pete's memory served him well.

Beyond the desk were large glass windows complete with a door leading to the outside world. We'd never felt so relieved.

The rumbling continued below us; it was clear the building was unstable. The glass windows were starting to shudder, threatening to shatter at any moment.

We made a run for it, pushing our way outside and running as far away from the destruction of Terry's lab as we could.

It was good to be outside again; the air was refreshing, the grass soft and soothing against my feet and our lungs felt cleansed as we breathed the clean air.

There was a sound from behind the building in the distance – the thrum of propellers. A helicopter hovered above the building and thundered towards us. I strained my eyes to focus. A pilot was operating the thing, but the other chair in the cockpit was occupied by a man who looked down on us. My gaze locked onto his.

Terry smiled and the helicopter was on its way into the distance.

'That bastard!' I muttered. 'He's not going to get away with th—'

'Uh, Jacob,' Pete interrupted.

I turned around to see what was wrong. He was looking at the horizon, in the direction of Perth. We were standing on the top of Kinnoull Hill with nothing but a small dirt road that led down to the motorway which was our only way down.

The view was spectacular: the river flowed through its natural current; traffic on the motorway went to and fro, and Perth stood in all its glory.

Pete was distraught, and I sympathised as he pointed in the direction of the small town of Broxden Point.

I could hear it now – screams, the screeching of tyres skidding and the sound of a bellowing horror.

'There's only one thing that could cause that kind of upheaval,' I said.

'My God. What do we do?'

I stopped to gather my thoughts and to think of some sort of plan. 'We should go, we have to stop this madness, but we can't do it alone.'

'Who will help us?' Pete asked.

'There's only one person who can help us, but we need to find her.'

He nodded, 'Your mum?'

'Yes. If we find her maybe we can end this madness.'

'No one knew these things were being created under their very own noses, but now we do. So I'm sure we can help the people in the city,' Pete said.

'We can,' I agreed. 'I'm sorry I dragged you into all of this, Pete. I nearly got you killed and you saved my life. You don't have to follow me.'

He paused. I knew he still wasn't sure about me or about the creatures now terrorising the city.

'I know you're not like them and I'm with you all the way, but if those things travel to Newburgh then—'

'I know, I'll help you with your family.'

He nodded in appreciation, 'Thanks.'

We took a deep breath and headed off towards Perth that had turned into anarchy.

Printed in Great Britain
by Amazon

87557018R00210